OF DUST
AND THE RIVER

Design and Cover by Jackson Hager
Monroe Press
Eugene, OR
www.monroe.press

ISBN-13: 978-1-944533-06-9

For more book information, including sales, please direct inquiries to Tim@THUNDERMUCK.com.

Printed in USA

*This first one has to be for my Dad, Krazy Karl,
in return for so many stories that he pressed
unknowingly beneath my skin.*

OF DUST
AND THE RIVER

STORIES
Tim Hurd

You tell me you didn't sleep well. I say
I didn't either. You had a terrible night. "Me too."
We're extraordinarily calm and tender with each other
as if sensing the other's rickety state of mind.
As if we knew what the other was feeling. We don't,
of course. We never do.

-- Raymond Carver, The Gift

TABLE OF CONTENTS

BORN DOWN IN A
DEAD MAN'S TOWN

When the last passenger pressed himself into the back seat of the MUSTANG someone handed him a beer. "You hear about Olson last weekend?" he said. "Tara drank herself blind so Olson took her over to Kevin's and put her in the shower. Naked. The only thing she was wearing was a football helmet. Now, think about that for a minute."

The trunk was full of green bottles with hog's head labels, Henry Weinhard's Blue Boar Ale and tall red, white and blue cans of Bud. One of the boys had a key to the local grocery store. His father was the owner.

"Man.... I mean, SHIT!" said the guy in back, sitting in the middle. "Some guys have all the luck. That could never happen to me. I mean if something like that happened to me, I don't know what would happen."

"I know what would happen. You'd be grateful Olson gave you the helmet." The guy in the middle tried to smile, to laugh along with the rest. Then he told himself once again not to talk so much.

"That was last weekend?" the driver said.

"Busy weekend. Springsteen had a busy weekend, too." Springsteen was a nickname for the guy in the passenger seat. He always got to ride shotgun because his musical lifestyle inspired the most unknowns. He was dark and he had that strong jutting jaw. He was a drummer in a band, a real band where all the other members were over twenty-one. Everybody wanted to be Springsteen in those days, Racing in the Street, In Candy's Room, Born in the USA.

"Were you with him? So that's where you were last weekend? We were wondering where you were."

"Yeah. Me and The Boss. We were out for a ride, weren't we Springsteen?"

"Which one of you had to wear the helmet?"

"Very funny. It was your cousin Bailey wearing the helmet. You weren't wearing a helmet, were you, Springsteen? Tell'em, Bruce."

"Nah."

"Come on, man. What happened?"

"Can't."

"Can't or won't?"

"Won't. Can't. Same difference."

"I think the poor guy fell in love," the driver said. "Imagine, I was driving his mom's orange PINTO. Bailey had her sights on Springsteen from the word GO. I mean, SHE called HIM. See what I'm saying? If he knew why she called, you can bet I wouldn't have been there when he picked her up. But she called him. So it's a little awkward at first, me being there, but after awhile we went out to Ft. Stevens. We pulled the barriers out of the ground and took off down those paved bike trails in his mom's PINTO. By then, I was the one driving. In front anyway, right Bruce? That was a rush. Peeling around out there in the dark. See, we turned off the headlights so we couldn't be seen."

"You could've hit someone. Can you imagine hitting someone?"

"But they didn't. So life goes on. Go on with the story."

"Come on, Boss. You tell it, Bruce. It's your story."

"You tell it."

"Is it ok to talk about your cousin? Because if it's not, just tell me. Just say the word and I'll stop."

"It's ok. She's probably telling her own version to her own friends right now. She's probably telling everyone she slept with Bruce Springsteen."

"Hell, even I'd sleep with Bruce Springsteen!" said the guy in the middle. Everyone took a hard look at him, everyone but Springsteen.

"So anyway, while they're in back I turn up the music. You know, because Bailey told me to. And what happens to be in the tape deck but the COMMODORES, right? Singing 'Once, Twice, Three Times A Lady.' From that moment on Springsteen was doomed. He fell in love right there. Lock, stock and barrel."

"Cousin Bailey doesn't fall in love."

"You tell him that. That's what I told him."

"Bruce. I'm sorry to tell you but...."

"I heard you."

The driver plugged in the COMMODORES cassette. Bruce began hammering out the opening beat with his hands on the dashboard, closing his eyes like he was back in the PINTO again. The three guys in back started to sing along with the COMMODORES.

"I looove you. I waaant you. I nee-eed you. You're three tiiimes a la-a-dy...."

"Knock it off you guys," The Boss said, but he was smiling. They could see him smiling in the reflective glow of the green and red light from the stereo.

"Man, why doesn't that stuff ever happen to me?" the guy in the middle said again.

"Because you'll always be the one sitting in the middle or wearing the helmet."

"Shit!" said the guy in the middle. He was always getting picked on. Sometimes this bothered him but most times it didn't.

"If you hadn't been listening to that damned ballad you wouldn't be so cow-eyed and broken hearted, Bruce."

"Yeah, like if you were listening to 'Brick House' instead of 'Three Times A Lady' you'd be feeling a whole lot different." The driver fast forwarded the tape to the other song and the back-seat entourage started singing again.

"The clothes she wears, the sexy ways, make an old man wish for younger days, yeah. She knows she's built and knows how to please...."

"Now that's better. Isn't that better, Boss? You're not so broken-hearted now, are you?"

"You're not helping."

"Then you're a lost cause."

Privately they called themselves The Filthy Five, a title that brought on fits of false bravado that they mostly kept to themselves. It was a name they came up with after getting high and watching a Clint Eastwood movie called, *The Good, The Bad and The Ugly.* Mostly their courage came from the good fortune of not suffering the brunt of their own mistakes when they were together. They thought that together they could pass through the better part of hell, an exhibition of uncanny luck overcoming dire circumstances, like miraculously coming out alive after speeding into an especially tight corner at 75 mph, the driver hanging his right tires just over the edge of the pavement inside the turn, like a train holding to a track. Or like exploring the dark underground mortar batteries that were built on the banks of the Columbia River during the Civil War--the concrete ruins that would last for 200 years--where they only had one flashlight between them when someone fell into a deep gun emplacement where one of the 10-inch Parrott guns used to be, a deep hole where he landed flat on his back between the tall metal rebar that could have impaled his leg or his heart.

Among them, two had his own car--the driver's old man had borrowed the money to buy him the MUSTANG because as a kid he never had a car. Two of the others got yelled at everyday by their parents because they wanted their children to graduate high school when they themselves had not. Then there was the guy always sitting alone in the middle with a new set of braces because his mother and father had always lived with crooked teeth. Together the five of them held 20 stolen condoms--most of them past the expiration date--yet not one had a steady girlfriend. But it was summer, they told themselves. Who needed someone steady when the beaches were crawling with hot looking girls looking for adventure?

It was the 4th of July on a misty Saturday night. The seaside towns were packed to the gills, rocking and waddling like gluttonous fish. Earlier that summer the boys had been closely followed by a truck full of guys looking for a fight. The truck was from out of town, all chromed up and lifted. The MUSTANG pulled into a small parking lot to turn around when the black truck followed them in. No one remembers what insult the driver of the truck cast out, trying to incite violence with the boys in the MUSTANG, also lifted high over shiny chrome and wide rubber, but they remembered what their driver threw back at the driver of the truck. "Well I think you're an asshole and you're full of shit!" he called back. Then the red MUSTANG lost the black CHEVY in the small roads the boys knew so well. The Filthy Five had become invincible.

They cruised along with the vibration of the engine under their seats. They could feel it in the floorboards through the soles of their feet. The sound of the growling muffler filled their ears while the beat of popular music leaked into their hungry hearts.

The last length of road taking them to the fireworks was a dark four-lane stretch of highway that had only one curve in it. On the north end the MUS-TANG was headed south. The music and spirits and hopes were all sky high for the evening. There was plenty of drink and the promise of sex was lying like a waning sun on the horizon and no one knew this was when they would feel most free in their entire lives. The sky broke into flashes of light and white smoke lingered. In this new night darkness sex and music and sex reigned supreme. Before they reached the bend they saw a pulsing red light bleeding toward them from around the dark corner.

Traffic was backed up going both ways. There was a car crash, but only one car. Then there was a large dark hump in the road. "Is that a motorcycle? Shit! Look! It's a motorcycle."

"It can't be a motorcycle. It's too big for a motorcycle. There's no reflectors on it, no lights." Gradually the traffic moved, and they moved closer.

"Probably the work of some tourist."

"God, I thought that was an ambulance. That's a fucking meat wagon. I mean a real one, a butcher. See the logo? Who calls a butcher to a car crash?"

"It looks like an animal."

"God...I think it's a horse."

"My cousin hit a moose once. She was driving her DODGE CHARGER through Idaho. She said if she had a taller car the moose would've gone through the windshield and killed her."

"A moose? Where again?"

"Idaho."

"What possesses somebody to hit a horse? Or a moose? Rather than stopping or steering around it, for fuck's sake? People are just dumb."

"You think it's hard to do. To hit something like that with your car. You think it's impossible, till it happens to you. I was with my dad once when a deer jumped onto our windshield--we never saw it coming. It happened so fast, so fast there's nothing we could do about it."

"But still.... Come on.... A horse?"

"It never happens when you expect it. I mean, who drives down the road looking all the time for horses in the road? That stand right up ten twelve feet tall in your headlights? Nobody, that's who. It just happens. You never see that type of thing coming."

"What kind of car is that?"

"It's hard to tell. Looks like it could be a truck. A small truck."

"If it's a truck no one's walking out alive."

"Doesn't matter what it was. Look't it now."

"I bet it was the fireworks. Our dogs hate them. They shiver and hide under the bed. I bet fireworks spooked the horse and it jumped out of its pasture.

It's so dark. No, it ran through the wire fence. I can see it all happening in my head."

"Me too. Do you see the horse standing up in the road? I do. I see a horse standing up and that truck sweeps under it and the horse comes right down on top of it. Can you imagine that? Can you see that?"

"I can see it."

"I see it, too."

"I can't quit seeing the butcher. Imagine getting *that* call."

"Do horses scream? I wonder if the horse screamed when it was standing up? Before it was hit? I hear it screaming."

"I hear it, too. It's awful. The screaming goes straight up in the air like a search light that disappears."

They all look into the sky and as they do the images of the horse shrink and drain from the windows and the rearview mirrors. The flashing lights recede like a passing flood. One of the boys had the good sense to change the subject, to force the images temporarily from their heads.

"So what's a commodore, anyway?"

"It's a bird, a large bird with a huge wingspan. The largest bird in North America. But they're going extinct."

"You're talking about a California condor. A commodore isn't even a bird."

"Let's just play some Springsteen," the drummer said.

"I remember something flying on the album cover, in the sky, like a bird."

"It's not a bird."

"Springsteen, Springsteen," Springsteen said.

"A commodore is an officer's rank in the navy."

"No it's not," the driver said. "Not tonight it's not. Tonight WE are the commodores. Nothing more, nothing less." Then the drummer turned the music up till they could feel it beating in their hearts. Full blast. As high as they could go. Till they all could see the sounds that they made.

GRACELAND

Thin gauzy curtains filled with light were billowing in, as shear, as blue and golden as a cicada's wings, yet he stood sweating and morose. He could feel his discomfort trickling like a shallow brown branch of the Mississippi down his body. His clothing was soaked by the heat of the Mississippi Delta. He'd never been to Memphis before. Standing now in front of the thermostat, still holding to a piece of their luggage, he discovered that the air conditioning didn't work. In his frustration he threw the suitcase onto the bed on his way to bring in another. He knew he would turn around and leave, if he only could, but she remained joyful despite his misery. She knew how to relax into the heat. She knew how not to fight it, how to let it hang on her like a thin slippery garment. The trip had been her idea and right now she was trying not to listen to him. She was walking toward the opened windows hoping to see Elvis Presley Boulevard and the guitar shaped swimming pool that she'd seen in the online brochure.

Inside, the man was filling the bath. Outside, in the park, dark human shapes bent like pythons rested along the thick dark arms of a Bald Cyprus. There were smaller, flowering, Southern Magnolia trees, their blossoms standing up boldly against the heat. There was the sound of a western steel guitar, a piano accordion and a washboard leaking something by Paul Simon out from beneath the shade.

And I see lo-osing love
Is like a window in your heart,
Everybody sees you're blo-own apart,
Everybody feels the wind blow....

The one singing and playing the guitar looked up at her standing in the window. She waved and smiled and stepped back into the room hoping the man bathing would muster up guts enough to try.

They'd been together for a year. One year. This trip was to celebrate their anniversary and to give them something they both wanted to hold onto. She hadn't told him yet that she was searching for a song. She'd learned there was no way to pull him from his misery. She had to coax him out. She had to lead him into believing that happiness was his own idea. Ordinarily she hated this in people, this ordinary state of gloom. But something bound them, something unremarkable. So unremarkable that she didn't even know what it was. She was hoping to find it there in Memphis in some other sparkling form, something with music, some holding fabric that could bind them.

"There's no damned hot water either," he says from behind the bathroom door.

"Do you really want hot water? You don't want hot water," she says.

"No. But there should be hot water."

"Maybe the no air conditioning and the no hot

water cancel each other out."

"We should at least have hot water."

"You'd think so," she says, trying to agree, doing what she can to keep the peace.

"Especially for what we're paying, to be close to some dead musician's grave."

"Elvis lives," she says. "He'll always live. He's not just some dead musician. And *we're* not paying for this, *I* am. It's *my* treat, remember?"

"Graceland and pink CADILLACS and...*what* is it? Fried peanut butter and banana sandwiches. I bet we can't get one of those for less than twenty bucks around here."

"Do you want a grilled peanut butter and banana sandwich? You don't want a grilled sand-wich. Who are you kidding?" But he said nothing back. She heard not even his stir in the water. "We could ride a paddle wheel. I think we must ride a paddle wheel while we're here," she said, looking at the What-To-Do in Memphis pamphlet on the coffee table. "It's called the Memphis Queen. Let's ride the Memphis Queen, honey. Shall we?"

"As long as the Memphis Queen doesn't ride me," he says.

"You're awful," she says. Then she imagines him lying in the tub, his head underwater, breath-ing, and not breathing. "So awful," she says.

"Plenty of people agree with you."

"We need to go see SUN Records. And Union Avenue. And Beale Street, that's a must. It says in quotation marks that 'they've got catfish on the table, they've got gospel in the air.' Honey, did you hear me? Honey? That sounds familiar. What's that from? Are you listening? Did you die in there?"

"Yes. Tupelo Honey. I heard you."

"That's not what I said."

"You know what I say? I say this hotel isn't worth a tiddly-wink. We should be closer to town for what this place is costing us."

"The closer to town the more expensive."

"I just don't see why anyone like us should blow a wad like this on a hotel room such as we've got here when all we'll do is sleep in it. Even then, you're asleep for godsakes. Who's going to sit in their room all day with their eyes open just to get their money's worth?"

"I don't know. I just hope it's not you, honey. I hope it's not us."

"I just don't see why it's so important to spend so much on a room. For example, we could take all we're spending on this room and use it at home to make quite the monthly mortgage. We could have a pretty darned nice house for what we're paying here."

"Do you want a house? Should we start looking at houses?"

"All in all, if you think about it, it's not like we'll ever remember more about this place than any other place just because it costs more. You saw the pictures in the brochures and it didn't cost a thing to look at. So what else do we get by being here? That's all I'm saying."

"Are you done? Please tell me you're done."

"What if I'm not done? What if I'll never be done?"

"Then we're done," she whispers.

"Honey?"

"It's nice here," she says. "Probably the nicest place I've ever been. The nicest place I've ever taken me." Now she's sipping on ice water while she reads about the different things to see in town. She sees her image trapped in each of the ice cubes that are themselves trapped inside the glass.

"And you'll be asleep soon enough and you'll miss the whole thing."

"I'm not the one missing things right now, you are."

"And you don't need to put on airs here, honey. We don't know anybody here."

"You're here and I'm here. Don't we know each other? And I'm not putting on airs. I just want something nice. I appreciate nice. It's not like I take things for granted. I want something nice to remember, that's all."

"We just got here," he says. "Nothing to remember yet."

"Oh yes there is," she says. "And it's not anything nice. It's not anything pretty. Like the first thing we do is fight over how hot you are, just as soon as we leave the airport, like it was my fault, like it was something I did on purpose just to aggravate you. And now we're fighting over this beautiful room."

"It's not beautiful. And I'm not fighting. Are you fighting? I'm just saying. I'm asking. How is this a good deal? You know all we're paying for is that damned pool shaped like a damned guitar. How's that fair? I don't even swim."

"When life's not fair you try harder. That's the reason we're here, isn't it?"

"Only you know why we're here. This is all part of your big idea. Why *are* we here?"

"To be here," she says. "To be somewhere else for a change, some place worth remembering. To see if we can just be here, to enjoy something without having to argue about it."

"Oops," he says.

"Ya think?" she replies, but he won't hear her.

"How long are you going to be in there?"

"If I get out the heat is going to drop me straight to the end of my rope again."

"You were wearing the wrong clothes, that's all. You were stressed and walking too fast. You were carrying luggage and you were wearing the wrong clothes. I brought you some light shorts and some flip flops. You'll feel much better. You can't fight the heat, so quit trying. You have to relax into it. Don't resist. Pretend you don't care."

"This is me we're talking about. You know my body runs hot. It's not something I have control over." From inside the bathroom the man's voice echoes out at her like something from a memory.

"That's what I'm saying."

"It's hot, that's what it is."

A lot of times she feels like laughing at him when he is cranky, but she knows it won't fly to laugh at him. But now she is on holiday. They are both on holiday where things are supposed to be different, so she allows herself to try her luck.

"You're so funny when you get mad over such things."

"What things?"

"Little things. Things you can't control. Like being too hot. I mean, who do you really have to be mad at over such things?"

"That's another thing. You know I can't swim yet the main reason you chose this place is because it has a pool."

"Everybody can swim," she tells him. "No one ever taught you how, that's all. I can teach you. Imagine if you learned to swim while we're here. Wouldn't that be something? That would definitely be something worth remembering. Can you imagine swimming in a giant guitar?"

"I can't imagine swimming," he says. "It's your trip. Don't work on me. Work on you. You're the one wanted to come down here. I'm only here for you."

"I'm talking about us."

"Do what you want to do. Really. I can do what you want to do, so you decide."

"Honey, did you go to that web site like I showed you, on things to do? Did anything look good to you?"

"If I looked up everything there was to do in Memphis we wouldn't need to come down here, would we? You know what I mean?"

"That's not what I mean," she says.

"But do you know what I mean?"

"I don't know what you mean, but I think I know what you mean, and if it is then I don't like it."

"What do you think I mean?"

She is suddenly bothered by sleep, offering itself as a means for her escape. "I just think...." She lowers her voice again. He makes her tired. Her eyelids are bouncing down like butterflies. "You're mean," she whispers. "Sometimes you're just mean. I see that now." She gets up to lay his clothes out on the bed then taps lightly on the bathroom door. "I'll be outside waiting for you, honey." She leaves the glass filled with ice water sweating on a nearby table.

"Where outside?"

"In the park our balcony looks over. If you take too long I won't wait for you."

"Then where will you be?"

"I have no idea. That's what I aim to find out." Then the bolt in the door slips and slides profoundly as she leaves.

Outside, another small band of men is lying in

another large pocket of shade holding to wrinkled brown paper bags as if that is what anchors them to the ground. Some are sleeping away the heat, saving their energy for the cooler evening hours.

Quicker than she expected her man is out of the tub and sitting beside her on the bench. But she refuses to look at him. "I feel like the history of the world could lie in this place," she says. "If only we could find it."

"Is there no history at home? It's been around as long as this place, hasn't it?"

"That's different. That's not what I'm saying. Try to hear what I'm saying before you say what you're saying. Try that."

"What are you saying?" he says.

"I'm just saying I can see better here. I see more."

"What don't you see at home?"

"That's what I'm saying--we can't see each other at home."

"Maybe you just don't like what you see?"

"See? That's what I'm saying."

"I need a drink."

"You have a drop of sweat, as gray as a rain cloud hanging from the tip of your nose." She has never not wanted to touch him more than this. "You see those guys over there?"

"The bums?"

"Look at them looking back at us. Do you think we're half as interesting as they think we are?"

"Half as interesting and twice as gullible."

"I think they think we're tourists who don't know what to do or where to go."

"And they'd be right, wouldn't they?"

"Wouldn't this be a lovely place to get married?"

"You want to get married?"

"I'm just saying, for anyone. Wouldn't it be nice to get married in a place as big, as exciting and as colorful as Memphis?"

"We don't have birth certificates."

"Relax," she says. "It's just a thought. A terribly romantic thought. It's the perfect place for such things."

"I'm just saying we don't have our birth certificates, that's all."

"But what if we did?" she says. "Wouldn't that be fun? What if we had everything we needed? What if all we had to do was go to some justice of the peace and say I DO. Just tell him we wanted to be married like we were ordering something simple from a menu. Isn't that something nice to think about? That it could be that simple. To think like two people who thought they were right for each other. They wouldn't have to think about anything else. They would have no hesitation one way or the other."

"What good does it do to think about things we can't do?"

"But what if we could?" she says, and she thinks she can hear music coming up the street. "We need more good things to remember. Do you hear that?"

"I heard you," he says.

"No. Music," she whispers. "It's coming closer. Hush. I can barely hear it."

"I can't hear it," he says.

"Wait," she says. "You have to listen for it."

"I don't hear anything," he says, standing up suddenly. "And I don't really need to hear anything right now either. All I want to hear is the sound of a cold drink filling my glass. What I need is a drink.

A Mint Julep or a Hurricane or whatever damned thing they serve down here, anything cold with lots of alcohol," he says.

"You like whiskey," she says. "That's your drink, anything American. On the rocks. That's what you like." Though he doesn't know why, there is something about her knowing what he drinks that delights him in some small way.

"Are you coming with me? Let me buy you a Mint Julep."

"No," she says. "I don't like mint." Then, after knowing they had parted and didn't need to say anything else, she says, "There's a song for everyone, you know? That's what I think. What do you think?"

"I don't think I know what you're thinking. In fact, since we got here, I don't even know you."

"I think we have a song and I think it's here and I think we'll find it if we try. It's the only way to find it. It's here somewhere. I know it. Up until we leave we have to look for it. And who knows, maybe looking for it will be enough. If we do it together."

"Enough for what? What are you saying?"

"Just keep searching till we run out of time. But we need to get going. We need to get started."

"We didn't need to come all this way just to look at songs. We have music at home. You have all those albums you don't listen to at home. Songs are the same everywhere."

"I won't believe that. It's not the same."

"Why not? The music is the same."

"But we're not the same. We're not the same, at all. We're different here from who we are at home. Or at least I hoped we could be. I'd hoped we'd be different when we got here."

"Different? You've certainly been different."

"I need to know we can be different if that's what we want."

"What good would that do?"

"I don't want to keep being who we've been," she says.

"If there's supposed to be something good buried in what you're saying I don't see it. It all sounds bad. You're saying we're not who you want us to be, so what are you saying?"

"That we can be."

"I need a drink," he says, and he walks away. That's what he said and that's when he walked away.

Not long after he'd gone the group of musicians lying in the Cyprus tree started tuning their instruments. The drinkers with the brown paper bags were still lying on the ground in the shade of the Banyan tree. The musicians were still held up in the Cyprus tree. The guitar player dropped out of the tree like fallen fruit. He began walking toward the woman seated alone on the bench, looking down between her feet at the ground. When she hears the sound of his guitar she looks up. The guitarist seems to be walking toward her. He is wearing blue suede shoes and singing a tune by Marc Cohn.

Then I'm walking in Memphis
Walking with my feet ten feet off of Beale
Walking in Memphis
But do you really feel the way I feel...

He was timing the delivery of his song to match the distance from him to the girl. When he finished singing he was standing at her feet.

"I'm sorry," she says. "I don't have any money."

"Pardon me, cher. I don't want any money. You been with that cat for long, have you?"

"A year. One year tomorrow."

"Anything I can play for you to help you feel better by tomorrow? You like the blues? You like Paul Simon, mon coeur? He has a very good, uplifting song about the blues. You look like you like Paul Simon." He sits on the ground in front of her, his steel guitar lying across his lap.

"Who doesn't like Paul Simon?"

"This one is even Paul Simon's favorite. It goes like this," he says, then his whole body comes to life. He starts to strum and slap and knock upon his silver guitar.

The Mississippi Delta
Was shining like a National guitar
I am following the river
Down the highway
Through the cradle of the Civil War....

"Do you think you could put my name in there somewhere?"

"What name?"

"Cher, or mon cher. I like what you call me. That's me."

"Yes, mon cher."

"Good. I like that. And something about the Delta Queen, and walking down Beale Street in Memphis looking for SUN Records."

"And your friend? What about him?"

"Him? What about him? I feel like I'm in the middle of something new. Like I'm learning how to swim all alone inside this giant guitar.

CONTINENTAL
SHELF

Right now this is how it looks. The car is parked just above the high water mark where all the jellyfish and crab and other dead sea animals lay in a line. All the doors and windows are open to allow the water to break in from behind. Corrosive, salty seawater. The car is at a standstill but it's rocking in its tread marks, huffing slowly. It's in REVERSE, not PARK. Soon it will break free from the soft sand. I begin to walk away, moving down the beach.

I've been here before. Waiting for one of my father's cars to run into the ocean. The last time this happened I was also living at home, at my old man's home. In fact, it was my birthday. My father gave to me for my 16th birthday his brand new car to drive for one whole day. I didn't even have a license. In exchange I had to comply with two requests. I was not to receive any traffic citations, and the car was not to be returned. Ever. The main difference this time is that he wants to watch.

He's got me where he wants me, my father has. I'm out of work again and I'm separated from my wife. So I'm back at his house. It's the first time

I've seen the old man smile since my last separation which ended in divorce. Right now he's wandering up in the beachgrass pretending to be looking for something. His plan is straight and simple. My job is to dump his car into the surf and let the insurance pay it off. One thing about my old man, he's always had good insurance.

Finally the car starts to go. I don't know if I'm supposed to be dramatic about this or not—maybe clutch my hands to my chest and scream bloody murder. So I just watch. The car crunches and squishes over crab shells and jellyfish. It's gaining some good momentum, following the sandy open plain of least resistance. My old man is far up in the grass above the beach. Safe. Walking with a stick he's picked up in the dunes.

But two guys passing by in separate cars see this one rolling by itself and they jump out to chase it. One trips on his feet and falls down laughing. The other one catches up to the opened door. He jumps behind the wheel just as the car reaches the water's edge. The tires peel through the yellow ocean foam. I have heard the soft bubble of a submerged tailpipe before. He drives the car out before the surf can dig the sand from beneath the tires. My old man comes running as best he can, waving his stick, wobbling on legs that are thin and brittle as a shorebird's.

The one who fell now has a large bullwhip kelp in his hands. Its bright orange color has turned brown and it's about 20 feet long. Now he's sitting on the hood of the car as the other guy cuts cookies in the sand to celebrate the conquest, a bucking bronco and a rodeo rider. A victory dance. Now they're both laughing. So am I. They haven't seen my old man yet.

"YOU BOYS! GET THE HELL OUTA MY CAR!"

he yells. He screeches like a bird protecting its nest. His elbows are raised high beside him like wings. They stop the car away from him, understanding he might poke them in the eye with his stick.

"YOU BOYS! WHAT THE HELL YOU THINK YOU'RE DOING WITH MY PROPE'TY!"

The driver tries to explain but the old man won't listen. They don't know if he saw them save his car or not, and he doesn't care what they saw. In his mind it's never his time to be grateful. In his mind there are only different degrees of anger, and if he feels anything else it is from the pain of being out of breath. His mouth is open, his teeth are bared, he bites at the wind for air then throws his stick down beside the car when he's ready to crawl in and slams the door. He guns the engine and returns the station wagon to its original position. The one who had been driving the car picks up the stick but does not follow the old man up the beach.

Now the old man is pointing at the other two and yelling at me, but I'm closer to the other two than I am to the old man. The engine is now turned off but I know he left the keys in the ignition. He's ready to begin round two. The one with the stick comes over to me. He has questions. The old man is stomping his way back up into the grassy dunes.

The one with the seaweed now also holds the stick while the other asks me why the old man was yelling at me. Looks like I have to talk to him so it looks like I have to lie.

"He must have thought we were all together," I say.

The guy with the stick and the seaweed is named Eddy. The one who saved the car is Lee. They aren't in a hurry to leave. So we stand around spitting, not saying much. Just toeing the sand, turning over broken shells.

"You weren't even close to the car," Eddy tells me. He has a menacing tone. "What'd he say? I couldn't hear."

"I can't understand him either" I say, and that's not a lie. "He's pretty batty," I continue. "Pretty upset. I think he's out of his head." Lee faces me with a look that is hard, as if he is pressing me for the truth. But I have nothing more to say.

"He's lucky we were here," Lee says. He asks me where my ride is so I tell him I walked in from the parking lot behind the dunes. He says he'll give me a ride back but I turn him down.

"Y'see how'e runs?" Eddy jokes. He begins to laugh. "He never would'o caught that car. Ungrateful son-of-a-bitch, that's what. Runs like a fucking monkey--arms out like that." Eddy doesn't change his tone or apply any emphasis to all the foul words he uses. For him it must be as natural to say *shit* as it is to say *storm*. He puts his arms out and tries to walk like the old man, he says like a flying monkey, and he crows. I could stop myself from laughing but I don't.

We all watch the old man wandering in the beachgrass above. Eddy is now down on one knee with the stick. He's drawing circles in the sand. Before long we realize the circles are a woman's breasts and he's positioned the bulb end of the seaweed between her legs.

The old man is staring down at us, as if he's forgotten what he's looking for. I'm the only one who knows he's not looking for anything. He's waiting. He's waiting for Lee and Eddy to leave.

"What in hell's name you looking at?" Eddy whispers. He's angry. He's probably always angry, even when he's laughing, just like the old man. Like there's no middle ground. No separation between love and hate. I start to think how they would have made an interesting pair. Eddy and my old man. Eddy instead of me. The old man looks at us like he can't hear, like he can't tell us apart. He probably can't. Eddy walks toward the old man. I follow. Eddy carries both the stick and the seaweed.

"Where you going?" I ask. Eddie shakes the stick like he's strangling it.

"To return this to that ungrateful son-of-a-bastard."

"He's old," I say.

"Why don't you leave it in the car," Lee says. "Besides, I don't think he meant to keep it." Lee could be the smartest guy out here.

"That old man needs a lesson in manners. Maybe I'll just drive his fucking car back into the ocean where it belongs."

"Maybe you should," I say.

"Not a good idea," Lee says. I was right about Lee. "Who's your friend?" Lee asks Eddy, but he's looking at me. He's either trying to divert Eddy's attention or trying to catch me off guard. "In the car?"

"That? That would be my wife," Eddy says. But he says it like a good liar trying to come across like a bad one. Finally he throws the stick away, as far toward the old man as he can, then we walk back to Lee. Surprisingly Eddie does have a girl in his car. She can't be his wife though. I'm beginning to wonder how full of shit Eddy really is. Full of anger, piss and vinegar. Eddy's got to be pushing forty, though it wouldn't surprise me to know he's even older. It shows in his hands and neck. In the cannon ball belly that teeters over the edge of his belt, as if it could fall on his toes at any moment. He's obviously no athlete. He lacks physical grace. His movements like his thoughts are erratic, unpredictable. He jerks and stumbles and drags his feet. He's the one who fell down then got up with a vengeance.

"Well," Lee says, "does your wife have a name?" Eddy's playing with the bull kelp, wriggling it like a snake, his own mouth hanging open now--not like he wants to breathe but like he wants to be fed. He's getting uglier by the minute.

"Good question," he says. "Hey, WIFE! You got a name!"

"Who's asking?" she yells back. "Asshole!" Immediately she turns the music up loud enough to drown all our voices. I bet she likes to hear John Cougar singing "Hurts So Good" a lot more than she likes to hear Eddy's lies. So would I. This has to be Eddy's music, his attempt at trying to make the girl believe they are meant for one another because he was her age when the song became popular in the eighties. Her head is rocking but we're too far apart to see if her lips are moving.

"She loves me," Eddy says. She probably does. Women amaze me sometimes.

With one finger Eddie fishes through the button fly in his jeans like he's going after a peanut caught in the back of his mouth. He begins to urinate on his sand sketch, rolling his hips at the girl in the car. She honks the horn. The old man looks up to find Eddy relieving himself.

The girl turns the music down again. "Must be colder out there than I thought!" she yells. She's not laughing. I wonder if she knows Eddy well enough to make fun of his penis. I bet she knows his penis a lot better than she knows Eddy. Suddenly the beach seems too quiet even though the ocean has begun to roar.

Eddy sees the old man watching. "You looking for a place to pee, old man?" he yells. "She's over here!"

"YOU KEEP THE HELL OUTA MY CAR!" the old man yells, standing as squarely as he can, stretching against the heavy curve in his back. Eddie swings the bullwhip around his head almost hitting Lee who acts like he didn't notice. I'm beginning to think Lee wouldn't say SHIT if he had a mouthful.

"Keep the hell out of your car…" Eddy repeats, in a calm voice that I know is only meant to cover his violence. "Should've done just that," he whispers. Eddy flips the bird over his shoulder at the old man. "Too bad it's too late."

The old man yells something back that no one can hear. The wind has come up off the ocean over our backs. It's blowing over the foredunes and into the old man's face, shocking his hair which is as thin and white as goose down. The sun has become hot on our heads and the sharp agitated voices of northern terns peel like lightening through the marine air that is so thick with salt it dusts our skin. The old man heads farther back into the sand dunes. He's looking down. He's found another stick. The pointed beachgrass must be piercing through his loose cotton pants. It must be poking into the soft white flesh of his thighs. Eddy starts to go after him. This time he's going all the way. The girl gets out of the car. I start to walk after Eddy who lets the long rope of kelp trail behind him like a rat dragging its tail. He holds his hand up for me to stop while looking hard down the beach at Lee.

Now the girl passes me. It's her turn to go after Eddy. I'd be surprised if she's eighteen. Eddy breaks like a stick from the girl. This is it.

It's a joust. A stupid joust. And a joke. Both of

these guys test their weapons against the sky, waving them like medieval lances out of control. Here comes my old man, pumping his legs, bulldozing his feet downhill and through the sand. He's got a full head of steam. His baldness passes through the dunes like a steel blue moon, his hair white hot and burning.

I don't need this kind of shit. I have a little boy at home. At my wife's home. I have a kid of my own. What I wouldn't give to be there right now. What I wouldn't give to not be here.

Inside my head is the dull roar of the ocean. I say nothing but from somewhere deep, low and mean, I feel a shift as if the tide has turned, as if the waves have risen up to wash through my body. They pick me up, holding me cold and close and carry me into the sea, over the breakers, past the 100 fathom curve, beyond the continental shelf where the bottom to everything falls away, where all land sinks beneath deep water, into the unknown. Just before I go under I reach up. I grab Eddy's arm.

ALASKA

Trig Thorsen was not the least bit surprised to hear the amount of salt in his blood was equal to that in the ocean. Trig was named after his grandfather, a second generation Norwegian who had drowned while commercial fishing for reds in the glacial waters off Kodiak Island. Trig's father was a drunk who drowned in Bristol Bay near Egegic while running a set net operation--the net had become so heavy with kings that it pulled the skiff and three souls to the bottom. Trig had been raised by his mother in Astoria, a riverside town on the north coast of Oregon. As soon as Trig got his driver's license he dropped out of school and never looked back. He decided everything worth knowing could be learned through his skin, so he traded his senior year for a commercial fishing job that promised him from ten to fifty grand in his first year depending on how hard they hit them. Or nothing. By his reckoning there was no way to lose even if the fishing was a bust because one way or another he'd end up getting to know the trade, which could carry him a long way if he could manage to stay alive.

His first job started in October, mending crab pots for the new December season. On deck his main job would be to load bait cans with chopped fish heads and frozen squid. It was a grunt job for a greenhorn but it got his hands dirty, and all the fishermen he knew claimed the after-stink of fish smelled like money. Every man on every crew had to gain a foothold somewhere, anywhere. Find some way to get on board, then prove himself through the work he does. Better chances at better jobs came through injury to others. Hard work was everyone's skill and all the rest could be learned by keeping your eyes peeled and your ears wide open. A guy only needed a few strong work habits in order to succeed yet there were a thousand ways to fail. Favors owed might get someone aboard but everyone knew that alone was never enough to keep him on the payroll. It was the best place to make an honest living, where a fair balance of luck and skill could make or ruin you for life.

Byron, the captain, was father to one of Trig's buddies on the wrestling team. When it was dark and the seas were up and the whole world was rocking in the flood lights, when there was no horizon to focus on, it was impossible for Trig to hold in his nausea. The winds howled and pushed into his back. The rain slashed through every gap in his new rain gear. He fought to keep his feet and hold his ground. Trig knew it wasn't hard to fill bait cans. It wasn't the work that proved itself challenging, not so much as doing the work in all manner of poor conditions, conditions that most sane men found to be physically impossible or miserably intolerable.

After three weeks working rough winter seas day and night, never hiding in his bunk, Byron started moving Trig up the job ladder. It wasn't that the new kid didn't suffer from seasickness, he just wouldn't quit when he was. Byron called everyone by their last names and in no time he was shortening Trig's last name to Thor, the Nordic god of thunder, not only because it was an abbreviation of his last name but because there was no job that was too tough for him to do. By the end of the season Thor was gaffing floats and running the block by himself while one then another who underestimated the bait job came and went.

Within a year, after crabbing, Thor had long lined for white sturgeon in Trestle Bay, trolled for Coho and Chinook up and down the hill outside the mouth of the Columbia, and he'd spent two weeks filling in for an injured deckhand on a long liner out of Dutch Harbor angling for black cod and red rock. That was the first paycheck he had that wasn't entirely spent before his next set. That's when he started thinking about having his own boat, no matter how meager. Before long his eyes landed on a 24 foot Young's Bay gillnetter that came with a trailer. The seller took Thor's $1500 deposit to hold it. Thor asked Byron for another Bering Sea job if one came up and in less than 3 weeks he found himself stepping out of a small bush plane ready to go trolling for salmon in Resurrection Bay out of Seward, Alaska.

Of all the things Thor had seen during his first year fishing the most surprising to him was the shear immensity of the sky. When he'd imagined a job fishing what he saw was a boat upon the water, but the sky was so much bigger. A man really couldn't tell till his eyes held them side by side, one stacked upon the other.

After a short season gillnetting for a small

quota of silvers back in Young's Bay Byron was willing to let Thor go back to Alaska, for a month this time. He knew how hungry the kid was to learn. So Thor returned to Dutch Harbor to finish the season for the same blut who didn't only injure himself but had finally exposed his meth habit which earned him one way passage home. That second trip to Seward Thor got bit even harder by the fishing bug, harder than he'd thought possible. It pushed him over the hump from dreaming to planning about fishing on his own boat, the one that was sitting on a trailer back home in Astoria. That Dutch Harbor trip alone allowed him to not only settle accounts on his dory but to outfit her with the best equipment for both safety and comfort that money could buy, including a new pair of Helly Hansen rain gear, a new watch cap--to look and feel the part--and a survival suit which made him feel a whole lot better about doing what he was taught never to do, to fish alone.

Though Thor now had clear title to his boat Byron offered him a crew position with full share jigging albacore, then after that another crew share long lining for black cod and red rock along the 300 fathom curve, so he signed on for another year. That was the first time he got to see for himself what guys meant when they said tuna was "raining aboard," as if fish really did jump into boats by themselves. At one point they'd been pulling albacore over both shoulders for ten hours straight. That was when Byron told Thor his future was set as long as he didn't drown or change how he worked, and that's when he told Byron it was time for him to head out on his own. He was right on schedule for the new salmon troll season and he still had plenty of time and money to re-outfit his boat.

Thor took his maiden voyage as captain from Cannon Beach, launching the double-ender just south of Haystack Rock. He trolled her up and down between there and the north side of Tillamook Head, his feathers puffed up as if he was cruising the gut looking for the prettiest gal in town. When he reached the cove he turned about and did it all again. Every fish he picked up was like the first fish he'd ever caught. He quickly realized how different it was to work for himself on his own boat--how one's pride could float so high above a simple paycheck. It felt like something he'd gladly do for nothing. But it wouldn't take much fighting to pay the bills or to outguess the weather or the decisions raining down from NMFS before he was reminded that no one else let you work for free.

If he'd learned anything about the fishery working for Byron it was that he could rely on yellow eye being consistent off Florence and black cod could be found along the curve all the way to Alaska. Though he was not yet 21 he was learning to work and drink like a fisherman but he hadn't figured out how to get laid like one.

*

Just as it was Thor's intention to learn through his own skin he was not one to compare his skin to another's. And though this prevented him from obsessing on another's success, after a few short years of fishing on his own it was easy to see he would make no real money till he bought a bigger boat and hired one if not two crew to help him out, which prevailed upon him another view of commercial fishing, that it was yet another 'growth or die' industry.

His old wrestling buddy was waiting for a new boat that Byron was having built for him. While that was going on he agreed to help Thor run a seasoned but beaten up 36 foot north coast troller named TWISTER that had been converted to a long-liner. He was buying it from a man named Nils who'd been trying to hang it up for years. They agreed to a deal that paid the asking price but required the old captain to ride along till Thor obtained his operator's license. Nils held his trolling permits and learned how to make good money farming them out to others, which he'd found was a good way for him to take a healthy cut off their catch without having to pay for fuel, bait or groceries.

Getting the asking price was a generous deal for Nils, but still the old sot demanded half a crew share for doing nothing but riding along while eating free groceries and stepping on the tails of everyone within barking distance. Thor had saved over $20,000 that he willingly laid down as deposit, the real kicker being that there was no way to get his money back if he failed to pay off the contract anywhere along the way, which Thor, being young, only saw as extra incentive to make good on his terms. Byron's son Freddie, also a third generation fisherman, turned out to be good with the stingy and wily old captain.

Halfway through the second year of his wheel tenure, after Freddie had launched his own boat, Thor was set to take the test for his Marine Operator's License. A strong rain laden norther blew in earlier than expected when drifting off Cape Flattery. Everyone agreed to take shelter in Point-No-Point, but the seas were already so high in the Juan-de-Fuca Straight that they had to duck into

Neah Bay for cover. In the howling noise of the storm no one heard the old captain miss the gang-plank. After fifty years at sea Nils drowned right there in the basin.

Thor was lucky to find in the dead captain's sea bag what was dubiously known as the North Coast Garden Club Code, which was a list of words, mostly colors and numbers, that deciphered map coordinates telling a select group of fishers where the getting was good. So now when Thor heard on the radio that "The Gold one was at Carrot Chrome Red by Apple Bronze Brown" he knew to run out as hard as he could to those coordinates and when he arrived he became the fifth boat to plug itself well over the scuppers with albacore. On top of that, Thor found a note written in Nils own crip-pled hand stating that there were two gold South African krugerrands lost somewhere on the boat, weighing in at over an ounce a piece that Nils had tacked down somewhere on the boat for luck.

He found the first coin easily, in its traditional spot beneath the base of the mast, perhaps farther back than Nils could see. The second coin didn't show up till two years later when one of Thor's deck hands found it while looking up and trying to think. That's when he spotted something round glued to the ceiling of the wheelhouse under sever-al coats of shiny gray enamel paint.

By the time Thor had his license to operate his boat he felt as seasoned as the boat itself. When he returned from his first trip as captain he felt as at home above the water as a fish did below. Fishing wasn't something he thought about doing anymore. Fishing had become the most natural thing for him to do. Not because he was hungry or he had bills to pay or because there were things he wanted to have--these were all incidental to a lifestyle that was as true to him as he now was to it. He didn't do anything to feel a part of fishing anymore. It was natural for him to be who he was, and he was what he'd set out to be, doing what he'd set out to do.

When not fishing on his boat he was learning how to drink hard and how to keep a girl in every port, from Monterey Bay to Port Angeles, each woman as familiar in his hands as boat lines; so familiar that he could tie anything from a half hitch to a monkeys fist without opening his eyes. When he wasn't shacked up with one gal or another he lived on his boat where no woman was allowed-- that was rule number one.

Naturally most of his money went back into the TWISTER. At the end of every year he would be as broke as when the year began, but he carried no seasonal debt. It was the life in between that counted most. The beers and the bluts, the taverns and the tail. All hail. Pull hard comes easy.

Then one day he heard that Nils had a daughter so he set out to find her. When he did he began making boat payments to her directly and she was good enough to sign over the salmon power troll permit without asking too many questions, which Thor immediately sold for $30,000. This allowed him to put in a new transmission and a more fuel efficient, more safe and reliable Cummins diesel engine.

The boat had not been properly maintained for years. She had no working refrigeration but as long as the trip lasted no more than 10 days she held enough ice to get her through. He had two greatly successful years of fishing but the boat ate up every cent that had not already been sunk into groceries, booze or women--the latter two becoming progressively more expensive. Thor pushed the second of the krugerrands from the cabin to a place beneath the first, then he painted his boat yellow and black, renaming it the ROLLING THUNDER.

*

By the time Thor turned 26 he had picked up two solid men to crew for him, both older than he was. One he nicknamed Clean Gus who was the best hired help he'd ever seen. Clean Gus had lost his boat when he got too deeply involved in a one-way love affair with Percocet and Oxycontin. But now he wouldn't even touch beer unless he was drinking with Thor because he knew alcohol screwed with his better judgment.

The second crew member came with the reputation of being a charity case who tried hard and kept a good disposition. Thor kept him because he believed he understood him like a car with a tricky carburetor. He called him Green Gus, the one mentioned earlier who discovered the second of the krugerrands on the ceiling of the boat's cabin. Thor called him Green Gus on account of his never seeming to get any job done just right, no matter how many times he'd done it before. The guy just never seemed to tire of getting yelled at. But Thor figured he was good to have around for Clean Gus to abuse once in awhile, which seemed to do plenty of good for each of them.

The standing rule about fishing seemed to be that no matter how much money one brought in during any given year when the year was up your pockets were meant to be empty, while your head was meant to refill with new ideas for the coming season. And whether you were married or not there was always a bar tab, a gambling note with your name on it taped to the mirror behind the bar, and probably some woman other than your wife who was quick at getting into the rest of your crumbs. One gal in Westport tried to tell Thor how fishing was just like childbirth, how you had to completely forget about what happened in order to ever consider doing it again.

One of the first lessons every captain learns is that the space his boat occupies is a big hole in the water that swallows every red cent and greenback he's able to drop into it. On a different day it makes perfect sense that putting all his money into this hole is the only way that enables the boat to give his money back in the future with any exorbitantly generous amount of interest. Another lesson takes a little longer to learn--and incidentally teaches these men how to put their faith into conflicting beliefs--which is when they break a case of 'bad luck' open what falls out can be any number of things, like engine failure, shredded nets and lost gear, bad weather and worse crew, and like a storm these misfortunes can come from anywhere. There are infinite ways to fail which only makes success taste that much sweeter. So sweet it makes fishermen want to endure the worst of times over and over again just for another taste of success, and the only way to have success is to keep your gear wet, your licenses current, and your engine running for as long as the bank allows.

*

On one especially clear mid-October day when the sun was flying cool overhead, the marine

air had become crisp as winter apples. The ROLL-
ING THUNDER had been pulling lines along the
curve just outside South Bend, taking yellow eye
and black cod for six days straight but had not
filled the hold even halfway when Thor asked his
crew if they wanted to hang it up. They decided
they'd seen enough, so they pulled their gear and
were running home when just off Cape Disappointment they reached flat calm, blue sky and slack
silver water. It was as if they'd been caught inside
some kind of snow globe, but it wasn't snowing.
Not even close. They re-set the lines, dropped the
second anchor and buoy ball then drifted while
lying on the deck in their work gear as if they were
vacationing hillbillies on some southern lake resort.
That's when they felt a bump and were hailed by a
woman's voice. When they opened their eyes all
they saw was a blonde streak leaping aboard, as if
a spark had jumped from one boat to another.

Green Gus, always the first to react, saw her
standing between him and the sun and thought
not only that she was an angel but perhaps that he
had willingly died in order to see her. Clean Gus
just closed his eyes again as he'd learned not to be
surprised at anything he saw on the ocean. But-
-and as the young woman might have hoped--it
was Thor who was most affected by her presence.
When he looked into her gray eyes, before anything
was said, he felt for the first time like he was falling
off the edge of the ocean.

She held her hand out to this captain, her gold-
en hair blowing across her face. "My name's Ania
but my friends call me Onnie. You're welcome to
call me what you want."

"People call me Thor."

"I know. Can I give you a hand?"

The ROLLING THUNDER doubled its catch on that first haul so they sent the line out for another soak before steaming back in to port. Then the crew scattered like stray cats, each going his own way, except for Thor and Onnie. Thor had been flat broke when he left the docks to go out on this last fishing trip but he'd saved enough winning Scratch-Its in his ashtray from the Oregon Lottery to get cash enough for beer, and the next day he'd be able to cash his check from the cannery. They climbed into his big blue FORD and stopped by SAFEWAY without one thought of taking a shower. He grabbed a case of OLY and was hell-bent on taking Onnie out on a bender. What Thor didn't know was that Onnie was just as hell-bent on going as he wanted her to be.

"We've got to be done with half the rack by the time we hit the falls," he said, twisting the cap off his third beer. He steered through the dark country roads toward the rural area called Lewis and Clark, each trying to tell the other what they thought was still true of themselves. Soon they came to Young's River Falls where Thor turned off the engine. He rolled down his window to listen to the roar of whitewater sounding in the dark of night.

"I haven't done this since high school," Onnie said. "I haven't even come out here."

"Me neither."

"You married?" she asked.

"Not even once."

"That's a shame."

"Is it now?"

"Well, it would've been."

"For who?"

"Your wife."

"Is that so?"

"You would've left her for me."

"Is that so?"

"Guess we'll never find out." Onnie was not sure if she should speak her mind or not...probably not. But stating her opinion had become a serious habit of hers. "If you updated your rigging by using plastic ganyons you'd double your catch," she said, looking out her window. Thor grunted while looking out his own. He was not accustomed to having anyone, especially a woman, offer him unsolicited fishing advice.

Onnie spit air through her teeth. But Thor had heard her loud and clear. He just didn't want to talk about it until he looked into it for himself. His red calloused hands began to fidget. He explored the square ends of his fingers for he had become antsy but not agitated. Onnie noticed a cassette tape hanging from the mouth of the truck's stereo. She pushed it in to see what it was and the music of AMERICA put them back on track:

> *Well I keep on thinkin' 'bout you*
> *sister golden hair surprise*
> *and I just can't live without you*
> *can't you see it in my eyes?*

As was his custom for so many years Thor wore what kept him safe and dry and looks-be-go-to-hell, clothes that ordinarily had sleeves and pant legs roughly cut off so they were short enough to not catch and draw him into machinery.

It was now his second night ashore and the second night he would spend with Onnie. But this time he took a hot shower beforehand, and he shaved his beard. He looked in the mirror at someone he really didn't recognize though he was dressed in familiar clothing. Between his missing beard and not wearing the knit cap that had become such a permanent part of his appearance he'd made himself look like a stranger. He wore a stained orange camouflage hoodie that he'd picked up years before for elk hunting, which was now grayed at the sleeve ends that were cut off and frayed at the elbows. He wore black Frisco jeans, the thighs silvered from wear, again cut off well above the tongues of his scuffed slip-on Romeos. On the back of the bathroom door hung a stained Seahawks ball cap that smelled far more like fish than football, but he left that behind too. He had just enough time before his date to rush out for a round of new clothes. He hadn't intended that Onnie not recognize him when he took the bar stool beside her.

They met at the Triangle Tavern beneath the Meglar bridge. They decided to go bottombouncing with the current of alcohol flowing downstream, through the Workers and on to the Portway taverns. Then if they still held their bearings they'd walk the tracks to the Red Lion Motel and Lounge where Thor moored his boat in the west basin. They made it to the Red Lion all right, but both were fall down drunk when they got there.

After rounding up their stools they relinquished their keys to the bartender. Thor fell asleep on the bar while Onnie rested her right elbow on the back of his neck, having yet another animated conversation with Mike the bartender. Mid-sentence however she stopped talking. She looked into the mirror behind the bar to watch herself slip like a fish below the polished surface. Mike picked her up from the wooden floor and got help from the night auditor to pour them into a room at the motel.

By morning the blue of the river was wind-swept and clouded with whitecaps. After a full night of rain the landscape looked like the sky had drifted down upon it, covering it in a crumpled blanket, where the silver spilled out, filling the low places with bright blue pools that mirrored the sky above.

The white afternoon light revealed pink and purple scars splattered like paint across Thor's naked arms and torso, on both sides of his hands and over his fingers. His past was raised in scar tissue. Onnie had scars too, just not as many. She traced every one of his scars with her finger as if she was reading Braille, making guesses on what the scars might have to say about how they'd been received. "Gaff hook," she said, looking into his hand, pressing her palm against his. "A monkey wrench that slipped," she guessed at his knuckles. "Or maybe a glass window that decided to fight back," she laughed. "Crab pot. You were caught standing too close to the boom," she whispered, turning back his hair.

"Close. Sturgeon hook," he replied. "It was a crescent wrench not a monkey wrench. And the boom was when I hit my head after slipping on some frozen squid."

Thrusting her right hand before his eyes, palm up, she said, "This one about ruined me." There was a scar the size of a penny on both sides of her right hand. "Dad was being pulled over by a long line going out. One of the hooks caught him through his rain gear. There was nothing to stop him from going overboard. All I saw that could reach him in time was this gaff hook so I reached it out to him. Me on the business end. The force of him falling was more than I could handle. The pole slipped through my hands, the gaff catching this one here. When I caught him the sturgeon hook tore from his leg but he made it."

Thor rubbed his thumb around the red spot on her palm. "I heard about that. Guess I should've known you by the boat you jumped out of. You changed the minds of more than a few around here about women being bad luck on boats."

"It didn't do much for my luck. I'd been next in line to fish the Bering Sea with the Torpo brothers on The Deadliest Catch, but I had to pass. I'd hoped to splash myself all over the TV."

"Didn't Torpo's boat go down, top heavy with ice?"

"I didn't say my luck was *all* bad."

This was the morning after and each was unconscious of their lingering drunkenness. Though their voices were lively their bodies barely moved. Which is the only reasoning available that might explain how Thor was to make it out to Englund Marine Supply while Onnie was still in the shower. She was perplexed as to where he might have gone since his clothes still laid crumpled on the floor.

Only when he reached the cold vinyl of his truck's seat did Thor realize he was naked. Naked and numb and bleary-eyed, only able to hold one thought at a time within the fuzzy confines of his brain. And right then he was preoccupied by the thought holding to the plastic ganyons. From behind the seat of his truck he pulled a shredded pair of orange rain gear and quickly put them on. He walked into Englund Marine Supply, not remembering why the rain pants were thrown behind the seat in the first place. But everyone else knew that answer when they saw his bare ass hanging from a wide tear in the hind end.

"You have a good night did ya Thorsen?" Ron asked at the checkout counter.

"The best," he answered, trying to get Ron to look him in the eye.

Since it was well after checkout by the time he returned to the Red Lion they decided to stay another night in order to refresh their memories on just what might have happened the night before. Speaking the truth had never been a priority when talking to any of his other women, but with Onnie it was a necessity that compelled him to speak fluently about everything. He knew he was far from perfect, but he thought he knew two other things as well. That he was perfect for her and she was perfect for him.

On their third night together Onnie made this quiet confession to Trig Thorsen when she thought he was asleep, that for as long as she could remember she'd believed it was her destiny to fall in love with a fisherman. "I feel like I've been in love with you my whole life," she whispered. Then she twirled one of her ankles beneath the blankets like a small cyclone, her foot landing between his feet, finding a warm and permanent place to rest. In time he would understand she did this when she was feeling playful and turned-on. He nearly pointed this trait out to her once but then stopped himself, fearful that she'd replace it with something much harder to understand. She wanted him so much it made her feel like less than she was, and she was scared, so scared that she thought it reasonable that she wanted to run because she was afraid she'd lose him forever.

After meeting Onnie Thor's luck took a quick

turn for the better. Not only was he hitting the fish but he was landing a lot more due to the plastic leaders that she had turned him on to. The first trip he took after leaving the Red Lion he plugged the hold in two days then turned right around and did it again in two. He had to admit to Onnie that the third trip was fucked from the word GO but Onnie made it easy to forget. The trip after that was so hot and heavy that eighteen hours into it the guys were getting so leggy they began to stumble with arms too heavy to hold up anymore. They were getting edgy and angry until Green Gus pointed out that he was hungry because they'd been burning all day without a thing to eat or drink. When they got back to work they filled the hold and were stomping on hatch covers in no time.

Before Thanksgiving, six weeks after they'd met, Thor and Onnie officially moved in together, which meant he moved in with her and she became the first woman Thor ever welcomed onto his boat. When they met it was like having their feet trip on something unavoidable, something like destiny. They knew they were there to complete one another and no matter what happened next they were meant to stay together. Even should they try to ruin one another they would never fall apart. They did not need vows or spoken promises. The commitment they had happened upon their birth. Perhaps even before that. Maybe all of time had been building toward this moment, as if no two lovers had ever been so closely linked.

*

One night on the boat, just the two of them, when they'd run out to see the aquamarine phosphorescence that was lighting up the water, when the stars seemed both above and below them as fish darted through the sea in glowing turquoise streaks, they felt like they were flying. "Trig," Ania said, with stars in her eyes, "if anything happened to you out here I couldn't survive. It would be like living without daylight."

"You're living without daylight right now," he said, but Ania did not smile. In his mind he tried to argue against her admission. He wasn't able to say the same thing to her. There was too much life around them to even think about what it would be like without her. But still, he said, "I know what you mean. I feel the same way about you." He'd seen too many devastated widows of lost fishermen to think the same might be in store for her. He couldn't imagine the world ever surviving without her. "Let's not think about that," he said. "Not on a night like this." There was a warm breeze out of the east and the dusty smell of dry grass tumbled over the water. There was the smell of wood smoke from fragrant campfires stirring in Long Beach and Fort Stevens. The water slowly lapped and waved its reflecting light against the black hull of the boat and the moonlight began to lick at their sweat. Moisture sparkled upon their bodies as the moon's blue rays poured over their skin. Together they forgot about their potential for loneliness.

*

Clean Gus had become so capable and reliable, and fishing had become so profitable, it was easy for Thor to put a new plan together that should include him. He would sell the ROLLING THUNDER to Clean Gus. Then Thor would buy a new boat and take Green Gus with him, allowing Clean Gus the freedom to hire his own crew. Onnie inspired Thor in ways that made him want to do new things, to travel to places he'd never thought about going to before. They'd already been to the Grand Canyon and Disney World and New Orleans. They had plans to go to Maui to create more memories that celebrated themselves, and they still wanted to go to Alaska by boat so together they could drink in the sights and sounds of the Bering Sea, from Bristol Bay to Norton Sound. Even though the sky was bigger than the ocean it was Onnie who allowed Thor to see the farthest.

Whether it had been the booze or true love or the ebullient and overwhelming feeling of success that came from being that year's Highliner, or just the simple belief that everything he'd enjoyed in recent years was because he'd been with Onnie, Thor got the idea of buying another boat and naming it after her. They had bought their first house a year before, a small but comfortable 3-bedroom wood frame that sat on ten acres with free access to Young's River. Thor put their place up as collateral and told Onnie to be ready for the ultimate surprise.

When the boat was to be released from the builder he told Onnie that her surprise was ready and he was taking her out to dinner. The cabin was painted in gold, a yellow gold as bright as Onnie's hair. He blindfolded her and did not let her see anything till they were on the open water of the river. When he reached the ocean he took the boat out of gear and let the engine idle as they drifted. The wine was chilling while he held onto Onnie's feet as she dangled her long golden locks over the side to read her name painted on the hull of the boat, SISTER GOLDEN HAIR. The letters may not have spelled Onnie but she knew the boat had been named after her. They continued to drift offshore, mooching for winter blackmouth, moving with the wind, completely loose from the continent. They had never felt so satisfied, so together and free, so entirely whole.

* * *

After nearly a full year of fishing on the new boat and having only moderate success Thor felt a tidal pull that turned everything suddenly and unexpectedly sideways. After three more months he felt like his heart was drowning. A string of bad luck tightened like an iron choker around his neck. After two more years of suffering he was in hock up to his eyeballs. For the first time in his life he didn't believe he was going to make it. Life had settled into a constant struggle. The fishing had become lousy, and then it stayed that way. Each debt, for anything from bait to his own mortgage, felt like another 50 pounds of sand laid upon his ailing back. If anything, the smaller debts felt heavier than the larger ones. There was no enjoyment, no positive feelings from the benefits of risk and reward. Now he'd come back from his fishing trips with less than he'd gone out with because he was falling deeper and deeper in the red. He was always under pressure from the bank. He was always under their threat of taking everything away. *So what now?* That was what he was constantly having to ask himself.

In all his years of hard work he had only thought to acquire things, to coast from year to year because the future had always saved the past. But the size of his debt had grown too large to carry forward, nearly as large as his burden of dread. He had to sleep with it, take showers with it. He had to sit down and eat with it. The emotional impact became a force to reckon with. In the bay he hauled in gillnets that were empty. In the ocean he raised crab pots filled with seaweed and bait cans that had gone untouched. He dragged for shrimp but tore or even lost his nets on underwater snags not listed in his Hang Book. He trolled for salmon and long-lined for cod and red eye but could not recover enough to pay minimum wage to his crew. He pulled at his own arms yet they would not come off.

He was suffocating and he couldn't do a damned thing about it. He'd never felt so helpless and miserable at any time in his life. He'd gotten to the point where he was doing anything to kill the pain, not just drinking. He was starting to depend on painkillers like Vicodin, then Codeine, now Oxycodone and Hydrocodone, for a small and temporary feeling of euphoria--the same stuff he knew had ruined Clean Gus. But he ate them anyway. It was easy to get prescriptions. He'd had plenty of work related injuries. He'd just never used them as an excuse before. Onnie was onto him but she too, for the first time, didn't know what to do. She didn't know how to help him.

It seemed upon reflection that it had built up slowly, but then the bottom fell out suddenly. Not even the North Coast Garden Club Code had been talked about on the radio. He wasn't the only one drowning. Onnie tried to console him, to remind him that these lulls were to be expected, that fish numbers had always run in cycles with good years and bad. She tried to tell him that one way or another the bank would understand and they would land on their feet simply because they always had.

Then the bank took Thor's truck while he was fishing, which wasn't crippling because he still had his old net truck to drive, a 20-year-old TOYOTA flatbed with two-by-twelve sideboards that never let him down. Then the SISTER GOLDEN HAIR disappeared and he had no idea where the bank had taken her. His personal belongings, including a 9mm pistol, he found stacked dockside in wet cardboard boxes. Onlookers had as hard a time looking at him as he did at them. He'd been going over his options but his options weren't many, and they weren't very good.

Clean Gus was backed up on his payments too, not only to Thor but to the bank as well--for a loan he'd needed to make necessary repairs in order to keep fishing. He'd not made a payment to Thor in over a year, his first obligation being to the greatest threat, the bank. In Thor's mind it was just another example of how shit rolled downhill. By rights, he knew he could take the boat back from Gus, but he would have to return his equity and give Gus enough for the bank to release the title. Thor knew that anything with his own name on it was subject to be lost to his own lender anyway. Anytime Thor had such thoughts it made him flat out sick to his stomach and his mighty name seemed over-inflated. It had run its course and was no longer viable or deserved. He believed having to constantly hear it within his current circumstances did more harm than good, to the point where he felt he'd done something wrong every time he heard it. He made everyone refer to him as Trig again, including Onnie.

One moonless night Trig drug himself from

the couch and up the stairs to once again hide beneath his sleep in order to silence the voices roaring in his head. Suddenly, like a sneaker wave breaking over him, he was overcome with stress, and the only thing to stop his drowning was for him to explode. He didn't notice Onnie coming out of their bedroom, approaching him from behind to put her arms around him, when he suddenly brought his right foot back to plant. When he brought his right elbow back to load up for a punch to the wall Onnie ducked to avoid his elbow and tripped. She fell horribly down the wooden stairs. The sound of Trig's fist hitting the wall was like a gunshot that sent her tumbling. Trig hopped down the stairs in four awkward leaps to find her unconscious. She'd hit her head on the door frame and lay at the bottom with arms and legs askew like a broken doll, blood running from a gash on her forehead, blood already pooling and sinking into the absorbing carpet. He called 911 while searching for a dish towel in the kitchen to bind her head, then he took a brown elastic bandage to hold the towel in place, hoping to at least slow the bleeding.

When the ambulance arrived the walls and windows inside the house pulsed with red light. Two medics ran in through the door that he'd left open. The first thing they did was ask Trig what exactly had happened and they listened while removing the towel in order to look at her injury. Then they noticed Trig's broken hand but did not offer to treat it. They braced Onnie's neck before loading her into the ambulance and had the driver notify the police on what looked like a case of spousal abuse. By the time the police showed at the house it was dark and empty.

At the hospital neither the medics nor the nursing staff would allow Trig to get anywhere near to Onnie, which Trig didn't notice because they were rushing her straight into surgery. He tried to wait but he was told by one young nurse who seemed particularly afraid of him that it was likely they wouldn't know anything till at least morning and that he should go on home.

"What's wrong with her?" he asked.

"I can't say," the nurse replied.

"But you must know something? From your experience? Please."

"All I know is she's unconscious and can't wake up. She was hit by something very hard on the head. It looks like...."

"Looks like what?"

"You have a swollen hand. Like you hit someone." At first Trig wanted to defend himself, to explain how it wasn't he who hit her, that he would never do such a thing. The young nurse walked away. She got behind the reception desk to bar his access to her. Trig reached out and offered her his cell number, and that's when he felt someone's hand on his arm, grabbing him. It was a night janitor, one who had caught the scared look in the eyes of the young nurse. When Trig poured his dead stare into the janitor's eyes the older man let go.

"I didn't hurt Onnie," he told the janitor. "I would *never* do anything to hurt Onnie. She fell down the stairs." Then he let his number drop to the counter and he walked reluctantly from the hospital. Upon his return home the sight of the blood on the carpet was so shocking he got sick as if he was seeing it for the first time. He chased through his memory looking for clues. Every detail seemed like an absurd impossibility except for the lingering presence of Onnie's blood which forced prior absurdities to become real. The police of course were already gone. They were now looking for him at the hospital. Trig was trying to remember whether he'd actually heard the word COMA or if it was something his mind was making up in order for him to understand.

His cell phone was still on the kitchen counter. He had three messages. Two were from the city police asking to talk to him about his role in Onnie's injury, and then there was one from Clean Gus who spoke in a voice that was just as matter-of-fact as the voices of the police, telling Trig that he'd heard he lost the Sister Golden Hair. He told Trig that it didn't look like he was going to make it either, that they should join forces so they could at least go down together. "Sounds like we're both up to our necks in the same bucket of assholes," he said. Clean Gus had not yet heard of Onnie's accident. Trig knew the insurance on Gus's boat was paid, in accordance with their agreement. Trig's mind swung back to the present when his phone rang showing Onnie's caller ID.

But it was Melody, one of Onnie's old classmates, from as far back as grade school. "We're all down here at the hospital waiting and praying that Ania makes it. But you know what, Trig?" Then she drew in a long settling breath. "We know you did this. How else could you not be here? We all know this is your fault."

"Then you don't know anything."

"I know you're the one responsible." That part, unfortunately, was true. It was an accident, but even accidents are someone's fault, even when the results are unintentional. Trig wasn't trying to avoid blame. "The police are here looking for you right now, and when they find you...you're going to jail. For a long time. Because that's what guys like you deserve."

"I want to talk to Onnie," he said. Even though he knew it was impossible it was all Trig wanted.

"She could die, Trig. Did that occur to you even for a second?"

"Forget you," he said, dismissing her, wanting to say something much worse. And though he'd intended to hang up he couldn't. He listened to her breathing. He listened because she was the only link he had that connected him to Onnie.

"They're going to throw your ass in prison. Where you belong. Forever." That's when Trig had to finally end the call. But less than ten minutes later Melody called back. The tone of her voice had changed. "Ania's dead," she lied. Her voice now lacked all emotion. "You no-good bastard. You took my best friend away," she said. Then she hung up because she didn't want to lay it on too thick. She just wanted Trig to leave the area, to run away. She knew too many wives and girlfriends of angry commercial fishermen who suffered from Stockholm Syndrome and didn't know how to leave abusive relationships, so if it looked like Trig had run to save his own skin so much the better. That way it would be a lot easier to get Ania to forget all about him. Trig was stunned. Too stunned to react. He sat in the dark trying not to believe the reality of it all, but it was beginning to sink in. No longer were his thoughts flying at him like a barrage he could not control. He was starting to think, to sort things through. How could things change so suddenly? It was like something in between, something critical for understanding this, had been left out. How could Onnie die, just like that? Disappear, just like that? He thought he must be in shock. He'd seen people in shock before. But then his ideas began to screw in and tighten.

Repeatedly he was clenching and re-clenching his fist, using the pain of his broken hand like smelling salts to force his mind into the present moment. He was clenching and re-clenching his jaw, biting into his cheek, swallowing the blood. He rubbed his broken knuckles against his chin when they began to itch. Then, in the dark, against the wall, he saw pass a thousand images from his life with Onnie since she'd first jumped from her father's boat onto his. From the cupboard over the refrigerator he pulled down a bottle of whiskey. It was half full so he drank it. Then he threw the empty brown bottle against the wall. When it didn't break he picked it up and launched it violently through the glass of the kitchen window. The sound of a storm was growing. It unleashed itself and turned back through the broken window. He could feel its aching cold cut like death into his skin.

The wind was up. Rain and plastic bags and garbage can lids blew with the small white Toyota down the dark and narrow streets. When Trig left the shelter of his truck the rain felt like ice pellets shot into his cheeks. Boats fought against their moorings, their waxen hulls bumping and rubbing and squeaking, sounding like a flock of geese taking shelter from the storm. Cables were chattering against the aluminum masts of sailboats while flags whipped madly in the wind. Trig pulled himself aboard the ROLLING THUNDER and while the engine was warming he checked below to make sure no innocents were hidden there. He could taste the familiar dampness in the air around the bunks. He could smell the memory of mildew and diesel and bleach, which revived images of old broken dawns and smoking sunsets.

He tossed the lines to the dock and motored slowly from the shelter of the marina, joining the river's outgoing current before turning on the running lights. He lit no deck lights in order to conceal the boat's departure, then he plunged forward, bouncing and slamming through utter darkness.

On the radio the Coast Guard was issuing a small craft warning and projected the bar would be closed to all traffic very soon. This was not the weather that even bar pilots liked to work under, not when they had to be dropped from helicopters to the lunging decks of ships foreign and domestic, to take the helm and guide them across the dangerous Columbia River Bar. Trig pushed the throttle forward, plowing into the water till the bow lifted and the boat began its rocking hydroplane toward the ocean. The rise in RPMs made the diesel engine whine. Blue black smoke bled from the smoke stacks, hurling itself up into the night.

Trig Thorsen focused on steering toward the mouth of the river. The rain was blowing sideways to the sea. He turned off the wipers because they only added to the visual obstruction and the consummate cruelty of noise. The waves were tall and rolling, crashing over the bow, breaking into foam that blew immediately from the deck. He was caught within the conflict between ocean, wind and river. He passed by the white cloud of breakers that disguised the shallow dangers of Clatsop Spit. He was approaching buoy 10 where the jetties were just beginning their ocean reach--that's when the boat began to feel sluggish in his hands, growing less and less familiar.

At first he thought it was the storm gaining leverage on the boat, fighting her back, holding her down, but then he noticed the height of the water was up near the gunwales. Even the lowest seas were slopping over the sides. He did not notice when leaving the basin that the hatches had been left open to air out the hold. What he knew was that he was taking on water. He threw the orange survival suits overboard so he would not be tempted to bar his fate. He turned the bilge pumps on trying to avoid the engine being drowned by seawater. He fought his way to the back deck to find the open hatches. He threw them down and latched them closed. He would not give up. He would keep going till he could go no further, trying to beat the inevitable odds of being swamped and lost at sea.

Conditions remained snotty and waves were reaching 25 feet. The boat was crabbing beneath him. He could feel how urgently the wind and river wanted to pull him down. He looked for the emerging moon but it was still buried. He could hear the cupboard doors slamming below as groceries and dishes poured out due to the violent tossing of the boat. Repeatedly the hull rose then slammed down against the water. The engine was struggling and occasionally roared when the bow dove over the apex of a wave and lifted the propeller screaming from the river. He had not expected to make it across the bar yet he began to see by the new morning light that he was about to.

Trig Thorsen was remembering Onnie on the night they met, when they were at the falls listening to the songs of AMERICA on the stereo. He told himself year after year that one day he would carry Onnie to the sky blue waters of Alaska. *What would that be like?* he asked himself. *To have her there with me?*

The sun rose over his back, advancing toward him across the water. A widening stretch of curtain hung before him, the dark western skies that lay resting on black nighttime waters. He couldn't see where the water ended and the sky began. Toward Alaska there glowed the thwarted northern star hanging higher than the clouds. He would have to cross the heaving belly of the ocean to get there. He would have to ride the rolling edge of twilight as waves toppled over the side of the boat, pressing their faces against the western glass. He would find Onnie there. Onnie, who would wash his flesh in her flesh. Onnie, who would carry him always in her gray, watering, eyes.

GIRLS OF SUMMER

I'm still new to this neighborhood. It's a run-down mess and eccentric is not the word to describe how these people live. No one here trusts me anymore than I trust them, which in my eyes is a good thing--even a condition for my staying. It keeps us apart. Except for Linda, a 12-year-old girl. Linda has patience and an acute sense of understanding that I truly envy. She is a young woman and when she lapses into childhood, when her spirit succumbs to her body, she makes me laugh.

Linda tells me those on her side of the street think I'm odd because I roast my own coffee. I think it's because I haven't given them any that they think anything of me at all. She claims her mother only allows her to visit me because she thinks I'm gay. She tells Linda she would not be allowed over here if I were a normal man.

Her side and my side live together at the end of a dead end street, on the dark north side of a hill overlooking the last few miles of the Columbia River. This morning the houses seemed camped-out like dew-covered tents, fortifying the end of this road even as it slopes up and dies against the hillside. Here, the life that does remain is life that has been abandoned. The houses are old Victorians and no amount of paint or maintenance can save them.

Linda's house stands three stories high. The wood skirting has fallen away from the foundation, exposing many thin wooden legs. There are two like porches that flank opposite sides, like the worn ears of a much-embattled dog. Odd plywood pieces sorely patch the places where shingles are missing. Gray duct tape has been applied to cracks in three of the windows. Miscellaneous weeds, blackberry vines, and even a small alder seedling grow from the stuffed gutters along the roof. Stretching between a broken down truck and its dislodged camper is a clothes line which seems to have the exclusive purpose of drying women's underwear. The camper is half-covered with a blue tarp, which is half-covered with wild red ivy. Spent fireworks litter the street in front of the chopped lawn where the grass is overcast by scudding clouds of dandelion seed. And throughout this picture, like some contest on the back of a cereal box, are hidden the faces and tails and ears and whiskers of more cats than you'll ever find.

The pavement ends just before it reaches the apartment in which I live. I've been reading poetry, which I seldom do, and just this morning began to understand the work of Walt Whitman. I sat alone, early, scanning his poems, anxiously trying to find the right vessel for my somewhat randy disposition, for my general restlessness and need, hoping to find enough self in my isolation so not to feel so alone. This morning I discovered with unbearable angst that I am living an existence of waiting. Then an eagle flew stoically overhead, traveling southeast away from the river.

It has become the summer of rain. Last May the Oregonian called for rain through September, and so far it has been right. It is now 2 PM on this Saturday as I sit alone in my bathrobe in the driveway near my porch. I have been outside drinking coffee and reading since early morning. It is the first day of August and the sudden good weather has drawn me out. By 9:30 the black gravel had dried and grayed and finally both the feel and smell of summer had been carried in on a bed of warm dry air.

At Linda's house the good car has been loaded with all kinds of miscellaneous household items, including suitcases and brown paper bags filled with previously opened food. The car is a Pinto. It's "good" because it runs. Linda's yard is littered with dead cars. There is an old yellow taxi station wagon, a decaying Ford pickup loaded full of "old broken down shit," as Linda once described. There's also a VW Bug that the father tried to save before he left. But now he's gone and the dead Bug is here, as well as three bad Pintos. All I know by 9:30 is that the car is loaded and the girls are planning to leave. From the driveway I can hear one of them singing in their house. There are three girls altogether, and a baby about a year old that they just call Baby. And there's the mother, big and brawny as an angry Welch mare, who is always nagging about something.

The girl singing is not Linda so it has to be either Jeanine who is one year older, or Jonna who looks to be about fifteen. It's probably not Jeanine.

The mother comes out of hiding, beating her way down the steps and along the path to the car. "Oh Jesus, Jonna! Shut up!" she yells. "Just listen to her!" I'm the only one outside but I'm thinking it's impossible that she should be talking to me. All she's done since I moved here is to look at me from her kitchen window across the street. Not once has she made any attempt toward conversation. It's more like she just can't control her thoughts this morning. Or her mouth. "I can hear her clear down here!" she yells. "Driving me insane!" But Jonna continues to sing. I can't make out the words but then there probably aren't any. She's just happy to be leaving this place.

"I can't open the goddam hatch 'cause Jonna's got the fucking car keys!" Jonna likes to keep things locked up. She has keys to all the broken down cars. She secures her personal belongings inside them, including most of her clothes.

"You must want t'come home awful early!" the mother threatens, and she trudges back to the house. She walks like she's dragging something heavy tied to her waist. Linda is now on the porch. With one finger she waves down to me.

"Like *how* early?" Linda asks.

"Like NOW *early!* Like we're going to haul this shit back to the house 'cause Jonna's driving me insane! Get from Jonna, my adopted daughter, the goddam car keys. Would you!" Maybe she *is* talking to me, maybe she's trying to tell me that Jonna is not her real daughter at all—maybe she's trying to tell me that despite her loud and obnoxious voice she also has some kind of goodness I should know about. I raise my book of Whitman as if I was doing the same thing.

Linda tries yelling at Jonna to make her stop singing, but Jonna continues, louder than before.

"I've got to be goddam stupid to even THINK about going camping with you! I hate camping! Especially with Troy gone." Troy is the father. It suddenly occurs to me that Troy could be the father of all the girls, like Jonna could have a different mother. But I'm just guessing. Mostly, this family is a mystery to me. Linda gives her mother a reminding look. "And don't give me anymore crap about that! He's gone, isn't he! Can't you shut her up for a minute!" Just then Jeanine comes out and drops a bag of rice that breaks open on the porch. She's shorter than Linda. She's chubby and wears glasses and baggy clothes. Her hair always hangs big and ratty down around her face. Her appearance could be comical but it's not.

"THAT'S it! We're not goin!" the mother declares.

"Why?" all three girls question at once, all three girls knowing when to start taking the mother seriously.

"Why? Cause if you can't be good here just imagine how you'll be out there!" Jeanine shakes her head and disappears into a cloud of hair. Her arms hang loosely down toward Linda who is cleaning up the rice. Jonna has quit singing and appears on the landing with Linda and Jeanine. "Unload the car," the mother orders, but none of the girls even begin to move. "NOW!" Jonna drops the car keys into the rice. In one fluid motion she streaks down the steps and lands in the bed of the broken down Ford, from where she stares at the other girls as if she just jumped from their photograph. In the kitchen of their house Baby smears a spoonful of breakfast goo all over the window. Jonna smiles, but only with her eyes.

After opening the hatch of the car, the mother returns inside, leaving Jonna, Linda and Jeanine to iron things out.

Jeanine flows slowly down the steps like a landslide of mud, her head and arms hanging helplessly down. She stands beneath the Pinto's opened hatch waiting for Linda but Linda continues to stand where she is, saying nothing. "I'm not helping," Jeanine tells Linda, as she shakes her head and disappears inside her hair.

"Forget it," Linda says.

"I'm not helping," Jeanine says again, even as she grabs one of the pillows from the back of the car.

Jeanine seems to have the customary attitude of most children, one that is bubbly, spontaneous, even happy and naturally self-possessed. But she breaks down easier than most when confronted by obstacles, as if she were merely built with weaker fuses than other children.

"What are you going to do?" Jeanine asks, now hugging two pillows and peering out through the hanging bars of her hair.

"Nothing."

"Nothing?"

"Jonna's going to do something."

Linda, although the youngest except for Baby, is the family's emotional leader. Unconsciously she orchestrates these other bent instruments as best she can. She is the cook, the worker, the family conscience. Without her the family would be as fierce and unruly as the cats.

When I have given Linda even the smallest compliment she will sit dazed. She will stare off into space as if trying to figure out what just happened, and possibly how to make it happen again. Then she jumps off the couch and runs outside.

Jonna is still standing in the back of the truck among all the junk gathered there, just like another of those six thousand cats that haunt this neighborhood—risen safely above the ground, getting a higher perspective, preening and planning. The cats are always hungry; some are beautiful; all are dangerous to approach. I saw Jonna out near the woodpile last winter, shortly after Christmas. Shortly after I moved in. She was setting up empty beer bottles and smashing them to pieces with a thin metal pipe, showing no emotion--no anger, no pain, and no real satisfaction, as if she were hypnotically stabbing her own numb flesh. Her spirit is as wild as a feral cat's already.

A lone crow flies overhead, looking like the lost shadow of the eagle that passed by earlier. Jonna jumps from the Ford and lands with graceful ease next to the skeleton of a picked over Pinto motor lying on the ground. She knows her body better than the other girls. It shows in her walk. It is obvious that she has greater knowledge of her body's hidden powers and probably will use her body as a vehicle for freedom, as something to one day use to escape this place--a sleek car moving too fast through blind curves. When Jonna is around I cannot take my eyes off of her. Her grace is athletic and demands atten- tion. She walks confidently up toward the house, her legs smoothly striding, her thin hips and arms swinging.

Jeanine moves to follow, but Jonna stops her. "You stay there! By the car!" Jeanine does as she is told. All the doors and the hatch to the Pinto stand open, the morning dew now disappearing from the inside of its windows.

Jeanine buries her face deep within her hair, repeating to herself only barely loud enough for me to hear. "DEAD DEAD DEAD DEAD DEAD DEAD DEAD DEAD…" bubbles her breath as she melts down to the ground where she remains unmoving, as if she'd just drifted to the bottom of a dark black lake.

Jeanine is the one who captures things in jars—

bees and spiders and dragon flies, salamanders and frogs, the wounded snakes and mice and birds left for dead by the cats. Despite her efforts to save them not one ever survives.

Without breaking stride Jonna spits. She snorts in through her nose like a man and with strangely eloquent style pops out a wad of snot, lofting it off into the air toward the head of a flower that has crossed her path. In passing, she tears the flower off at the roots. On the porch one of the cats has squatted over the spilled rice, still and tense, only its tail twitching. Jonna swings the flower and smashes the cat like a piece of glass. Caught off guard it springs back off the porch, every tooth and claw exposed, while Jonna disappears inside the house.

Through the window I see Jonna pick up Baby. She hoists the child to rest on one out-pushed hip and waves Baby's cereal spoon at the child's mother. Or... perhaps Jonna is the mother. Baby's mother. I don't know and I hesitate to consider whether or not there are actually three mothers now for all these girls. Jonna leans forward waving the spoon, appearing to be a painter angrily creating some cruel picture. Then Jonna disappears from view, but less than a minute later she's out the front door wearing a man's baseball cap. Then I notice each of the girls is wearing at least one piece of the father's clothing. Jeanine is swimming in a black and white plaid shirt, which currently surrounds her unmoving body like a pool of tartan blood. Linda is wearing a pair of cut off pants bunched around the waist, secured with a thick black belt twice her size.

Linda steps over Jeanine's body to close the orange Pinto hatch while Jonna locks Baby in the car. Still hugging the pillows Jeanine claps her hands then rises off the bottom and moves to the middle of the back seat, followed immediately by Linda. Jonna, not yet inside the car, begins securing the doors and trunks to all the cars in the yard, making sure they are locked. She then goes to the window next to Baby.

"Baby," Jonna pleads tenderly. "Roll down the window." Baby doesn't notice her so Jonna begins knocking on the glass. Jonna knows how to flavor her words. She knows words alone are not enough to get what she desires. "Quick! Baby! The car's on fire!"

Baby doesn't care. At this very moment Baby is learning not to give a shit.

"Ba-by!" Jonna tries again, now feigning hysterics. "You are go-ing to die!" Jeanine reaches across Baby to roll down the window. Jonna leans inside the car, showing she's had the keys all the time. "SUCK-er-rrs…" she says smugly and goes to wait again in the bed of the truck.

Jonna is extravagant with her emotions. Excessive. Absurd. She is an actress, one who melodramatically overplays the hope and disappointment of others in order to kill her own feelings of hope and disappointment.

The angry matron watches from a window in the house, peering through the smear of breakfast goo. It's hard to tell who she's looking at. Ten minutes later she comes down carrying a can of kerosene and some newspaper. She yells to everyone or to no one, "Don't worry about it! He don't know what makes this family TICK!" Inside the car Linda has been brushing Jeanine's hair. Now she ties it back in a ponytail and without knowing probably begins to explain to Jeanine just how this family really does tick.

Jonna is the last one to enter the car, sitting in front on the passenger side. She rolls the window down, sticks her elbow out and surveys the yard. Without reason it enters my mind that the sun they're after is like the father that left them, and somehow they've agreed that he is worth looking for. But when I look at the western sky there are vast clouds on the dark horizon.

Out of the blue Linda dives from one of the car's doors and flies to my side. "Do you have any pop!" she cries. I remind her that there are some warm cans in the cupboard. I tell her to help herself. When she comes back, concealing one can beneath her shirt, I ask if she's happy to be going. She says she is, that it just takes awhile for her mother to decide sometimes. The pop, she says, is a surprise for her. They've run out and she's been in a bad mood all morning because of it. I am compelled to stop her once more before she goes, as if it is she who will never return. I call her name. She turns her head. Without forethought I ask her why she trusts me, as if her answer alone could somehow redeem me from my loneliness. But she only laughs, and smiles, then breaks into a run.

In a poem Whitman said women attracted him fiercely and undeniably. He said he was drawn by their breath as if he was no more than a helpless vapor, so strongly that all else fell away, including his expectations of heaven and all his fears of hell.

"Dammit!" Jonna yells. "Who spilled the goddam rice?"

"I did," Linda lies. Then she waves--behind her head without looking, trusting that I am here and that I know she is smiling. It is only now that I understand we are saying good-bye.

Wild geese quiver overhead, their wintry voices crying after summer's blue water, running their squeaky wheels against the sky. Their shadows cut gracefully along the ground, through houses and Pintos. Through hope and disappointment. Through the girls, and Whitman, and me.

FLIGHT

"There you sit, so young," you say, and your mailman is late. His short visit is often the brightest point in your day. Not that he carries to you anything of great importance. The only thing he ever brings of any consequence is your monthly check from the state, and this is always the same. This always gets spent the same way for the same things. And you don't feel you really have to do anything to earn it, so what value can possibly be in that?

Your mailman has been easy for you to talk to. You feel you can tell him anything. A portion of the trust you have born him is based on the fact that he never tells you anything about anyone else. And he *is* a mailman, after all. It *is* his job to keep things confidential. Another reason you have chosen him as your confidante lies in the fact that you do not know his name, even though he obviously knows yours. What you probably enjoy most about him is his cleverness, the way he plays with words. And the best part about this is that he seems not to take any pride in it. In fact, he acts as if he doesn't know what he's saying until you take notice. And even though it is he who is being clever you know this makes you feel smart.

When you're alone, and your six-month-old is asleep, like now, the monotonous ticking of the clocks can become so intense that you have to turn on the radio. Not too loud—you don't want to wake her. Just high enough to hide the beating. There are only two clocks, but each ticks rather loudly, and one seems to echo the other. You get lost trying to hear which is which. Something in the space where you go looking to find which clock is sounding first makes you feel as though you are going insane. You want to talk to him about this but so far you haven't found the words.

Your feelings for him do not go beyond the short daily exchange outside your door. You do not think of him in that way. Not really. Although occasionally your imagination takes off without you. It flies off on its own into the realm of slow-moving zippers and small metal buttons...but, it never returns. It all disappears as soon as you see him again. This seems safe to you. This seems okay. There are certainly worse things you can do with an overabundance of time. You know the truth of that all too well. Besides, who else do you have to think about? You are done with all that, for good and forever. You have other things to think about now.

Like the noise you've recently begun to hear. You can't tell where it's coming from. Whenever you hear it, even though it scares you, you get up and go looking for it. You always look first to see if it's the sound of the mailbox. But then you start hearing it at night too, and those things that are not too difficult to face during the day can be impossible to confront after dark. Standing over the sink, looking out the window for him, you cannot stop yourself from pushing your hands down beneath the warm dishwater. You try to hear down there, beneath the surface, through the tips of your fingers. The trick is to turn off your ears. Large soap bubbles reflect the plain room around you in purple colors, rainbow colors. But they burst, silently, as your hands move along the bottom. You want to tell him that even though you have hardly gone outside for six months you still feel like you're getting ready for something. Even though you're only cleaning house and raising your daughter and slobbing around the TV. Even though it's always the same person looking back at you from the mirror.

When you gave birth to your baby you refused all painkillers, even aspirin, because you wanted to know what real pain felt like, so that all the pain you'd felt up till then was not really pain at all, as if childbirth could make all that disappear behind the curtain of pain brought by your firstborn. So when your midwife told you to push, to push with all you had, you pulled instead, you pulled the curtains together with all your might.

The mailman   talks casually about members of his family, and gradually you feel like you know them. He tells you the story of how he spent a whole weekend clearing the drains at his mother's house, and he lightly chastises her for never fixing anything herself, and never hiring anyone outside the family to help her out. He says, "When my mother has to fix anything but her hair you know it's been down a long time." You think this is funny. You want to write this down and tape it to the mirror in the bathroom. You confess to him that you spend way too much time thinking about the mail, and he says, "You know, my whole life is like that some days." You think this is pretty funny, too. You do write this one down. Once, he told you, "Maybe you should just sit down and take five for a minute." And so you did.

You can barely see yourself in the mirror now for all the things he has said to you. Every time you find yourself in the bathroom you read at least one of the funny or kind things he's had to say. Many times you stand until your legs begin to tire. Other times you disappear then come back on the other side, and you stand there looking at the words passed between you, looking out at the blank backs of the paper. You try to see who is on the outside now. You become afraid of what might lay in the infinite space behind you.

You feel you are pretty honest about who you are and how you got here, to this house, in this place. "But what now?" This is what you ask yourself several times a day. There is still a part of you that wants to make something of yourself, but for the life of you, you just don't know what that is. It is not something you can talk about.

You still think you have the ability to do just about anything. Although you know, just as it has been in other areas of your life, that whatever it is won't be easy. It will be hard getting started. After finding what you want it will be the first step that is hardest. Like that day on the beach before Kealie was born, when there was no denying you were pregnant. You fled from the city to be on your own. You borrowed your mother's car and drove, stopping three times because the nausea was too great to keep inside of you. You'll never forget the moment you reached the mountain summit and began to smell the ocean, still forty miles from the beach. You'll never forget hearing the waves reach through your opened window and how they pulled at you with a force you could not deny. You drove the car onto the beach and headed north. Your window was down on the ocean side and you drove. Slowly along the whispering edge of the waves, for thirty minutes you drove. Talking to the waves. Thinking out loud. Not a single thought that went through your mind did not make it past your lips. Everything you said you unloaded, you threw out and drowned in the deep blue sea, and you were so relieved. You spoke in your natural voice and nothing was forced in any way. You were moving in a car running parallel to a flight of pelicans that was moving north beside you, in single file. They would ride low down in the trough between the breakers, so near to the water they could have left a mark, until their waves reached the beach, coming very near to you. Then they would jump over one or two more waves to sink down low again over the water, gliding in toward you and the beach again. Their flight seemed effortless and beautiful, and free. And so did yours.

They flew, you flew. You talked, they listened, to everything you had to say about everything that had happened, and you felt like the hard words and ill feelings were being pressed from your muscles. Like they were being combed from your hair. Rubbed and cleansed like sand out from between your toes. You talked, rambled, digressed. With the wind in your hair, the sound of the water in your ears, and the fresh salt-smell of ocean in your lungs. You left your old self to drown in the ocean surf, to fly away on the sea air, to bury herself in the hard wet sand. And you left her there. You had wanted to tell it, to lay harsh words upon it, and you did--you said it, all at once, once and for all, only for yourself and you did it and it left you and that's when you decided you would live here in a place that would take you as you were and let you be alone and leave you feeling through and through brand new.

This is how you learned to speak and to feel good about what you have to say. Until then you had not realized how much more you like to talk when no people are around to hear you. And your mailman comes by to remind you that you and Kealie are not alone.

Now here you are, sitting on your couch with your baby asleep in the other room, trying to find a sound that just won't quit. You get up to check the mail and your movement seems to drive the noise away. You return to the couch and pull your legs up beneath you. You pull your sweatshirt down over your feet.

You used to think about inviting him in, but then you remembered how true it is that anyone can go crazy. Without notice. Anyone can become violent, and there's just no way to know when it's coming. This occurred to you on one of those days when the clocks were too loud and you had no radio with which to cover them. It was before that other sound had started--thank goodness for that. It was when Kealie was only a month old and it was impossible to know what she was fussing about. Her crying was too much and your lack of sleep was too hard. Nursing was too uncomfortable and the isolation was still too lonely.

So you laid Kealie too hard down on the bed you did and you tried hard you tried so hard to hit her. You did. Your arm and your hand and your face and even your feet grabbing at the wood floor to hold you were all so hard and all you could do was stand there beside your child and you reached over with wooden fingers on both hands, your hands fighting one another, one hand pulling on the wrist of the other with your teeth gripped together and your fingers pinching tight like clothes pins and bit bit bit with those fingers until your whole body ached from squeezing the pink cloth of Kealie's baby blanket. The pink cloth of your baby's blanket. Just the blanket. So…no harm done. Thank goodness. And the sound of your weeping took you by the hair and pulled you from the baby's room.

You ran outside sobbing and fell into the mailman who listened and petted your shoulder very fatherly and told you that's a good sign for your becoming a good mother because everyone feels the same way sometime or other and few make it through without doing some harm and the first time's always the hardest and thank goodness thank goodness for your little girl that there's no chance for it to get any easier for you just in case there happens to be a next time because you see the first time still has not yet happened. You did not hurt her. And she will never know you nearly did.

Somewhere along the way you have taken it upon yourself to put the flag up on your mail box regardless of whether or not you actually have any mail to send. Who on earth do you have to write to? But you leave the flag up just the same, and when he asks about this you tell him the truth. You tell him you need to know someone has been by to look in on you every day. You tell him it makes a difference. He says he doesn't mind. He says he's happy to do it. And you believe him because you were the one being so honest.

Now that's the third time today you've heard on the radio about a little girl lost down a hole. You've never heard so much talk about one accident before. Of course you're sympathetic, but, don't most people have enough problems of their own?

You would turn the radio off but your problems without the radio seem larger, much larger than the problems you hear on the news. The thought crosses your mind to make a phone call. You begin to calculate how much it will cost to call long distance to tell them to shut up about the baby in the hole. But you are broke, and you haven't had a phone since you moved here. You pull your sweatshirt again down over your feet and begin to wonder where your mean streak comes from. Not the one that led to Kealie, that was an accident, but the one that allows you to think to tell those people to shut up about a baby down some hole in the ground. It isn't from any pressure that could be building from being broke all the time, you are pretty sure about that. You tell yourself you've gotten used to it. You don't even mind using food stamps at the market anymore because you realized you don't really know anyone here. No one can look at you and see how you are failing because no one here has ever spent two seconds imagining what you could have been. And you're a new mother for Christ's sake, so shut up about it. Being broke doesn't bother you.

No matter where you were or who you were with, you used to have to place the heels of your hands up against your eyes and then you'd relax under the pressure of your own soft flesh. You'd lean forward and let the weight of your head rest against the warm palms of your hands. In the darkness there you learned you could see stars launching out of your eyes, out of your misery and despair. But you haven't needed to do that in quite some time.

The mean streak that bothers you most is the one that surfaced the last time you took the baby out to a restaurant. Kealie was brand new and all you wanted was to go sit alone somewhere and have someone else cook dinner for a change. But the people would all stop and faun over the baby which was okay pretty much even though a lot of it was pretty personal, until you got your food. And then it still seemed nice but it seemed annoying too. And then it got very annoying when your server joined in so you put your hand down hard on the table and apologized for your bad behavior but you'd just lost the father to a car accident with a drunk driver and you're just not feeling very perky right now. Which was a lie. And then the head waitress overheard and took you back into a vacant conference space where you sat and ate in peace, feeling rather gleeful at first about the dark little lie that wasn't really at all true but didn't seem that far off and it still shut the world out for awhile.

Between the front door of your house and the mail box there is always the sound of the ocean. You do not live within walking distance of the beach but you can still hear it. Sometimes it is just a white noise, almost like static in the background. Other times it roars like it's coming after you. You leave the couch and listen into the ocean noise to see if this is where this other noise has been hiding. But it isn't there.

On the way back inside you see by the clock that you've been sitting in the same place for nearly an hour. He must be carrying a lot of extra mail, you think. He has told you that Tuesdays are notoriously the heaviest days of the week. Or maybe he's sick and someone else is doubling up, covering his route for him. Suddenly you panic at the possibility that he will never return, that he may have lost his job or moved away. You prepare yourself for the worst and you pull your sweatshirt down again over your feet. You think for 40 minutes, wondering how well you really know him. Then you hear the noise, and you try to listen through it to see if it's still quiet in your room where the baby is sleeping. Finally, you think, it's a good thing you're not waiting for something important, and you almost tell this to yourself out loud. You almost narrate your own thoughts. But the noise is still there and this time you decide rather than getting up to chase it away you will wait for it, so you unfold then re-fold your arms, and you uncover your feet.

Somehow you know that if you wait it will indeed come and there will be no stopping it and finally you just have to let it come and get all this waiting over with, but then at the last second you just can't stand it and you dive out of your body because your body is just not fast enough to follow you up to the corner of the room the corner over the dining table where you sit to read your mail you look down and you see yourself still sitting on the couch with your legs drawn up under you and your sweatshirt pulled down over your feet again and even to yourself you look so young that you have to remark aloud, "There you sit, so young." And when you do this the noise disappears and the radio disappears and even your missing mailman disappears for the short time that you hang there above the table in the far corner of the room. "There you sit, telling yourself it's only money," you say. "There on your broken down couch, broken yourself, broken as a window, broken as a promise, broken as your daughter's first piggy bank. Broken-hearted. No, not broken-hearted. Yes, broken-hearted. But not broken because your heart misses *him*...broken because your heart misses no one."

This realization knocks you down from the ceiling back into your body, back into the straightjacket of your own arms. You hit hard against the couch with your eyes open and your arms around your stomach and there you remain, very still, listening to the absolute quiet that somehow envelopes the ticking of the clocks. The whole place now sounds like it's under water. Until the noise starts up and you can feel that it is not quitting this time. It is coming to find you. It gets louder. But this time you can tell the noise is coming from within so you loosen your arms to let it out even though you know there's going to be nowhere to run. And besides, there's something in your bones that assures you that this is not something of which you should be afraid. So you sit, carefully listening, waiting to hear what this thing inside you has to say.

You forget all about feeling like a bird being chased by her own wings. You can't remember the last time you had so many things to say at once. You don't remember reaching up to stop the clocks. You don't remember leaving the couch to find a pen and a sheet of blank white paper. What you do remember is sitting at the table looking at the sight of a young woman sitting alone on her couch, spending her life waiting for nothing in particular. And you remember wondering how on earth anyone could let that happen without at least trying to do something about it. So you begin by loving her, and you begin by telling her on paper, "There you sit, so young."

STAY

My 14-year-old hangs his head over the bathroom sink pinching his nose, breathing through his mouth. There's blood everywhere. It has filled his nostrils and is already crusted on his upper lip and it continues to drip in a rhythm that is so steady it seems this is meant to be.

"How long have you been standing here?" I ask, and I resist my impulse to sigh. I don't want him to confuse the thought that I'm not sympathetic with the thought that I know he's done this on purpose, that I suspect he would have allowed his nose to bleed for as long as it took for me to notice, even if it killed him.

"Awhile," he says, his voice sounding as if he has a cold. "And I'm feeling dizzy."

"You're bleeding like a stuck pig," I say, to see if he's been able to maintain a sense of humor.

"You're the pig," he smiles.

"Say OINK," I say, but when he says nothing I know I've said too much. He's my last chance to become the perfect father. His two older siblings are already gone.

I look at his hand, the one draped over the

edge of the sink, the one not pinching his nose. It's now shaking more than it was before I came into the room, or at least it's shaking more than his other hand. When he was younger, when his mother and I were still together and fighting over everything, I thought he would grow up to become a hypochondriac. Not that I ever told him this. In fact I've made it a point to caution him against labeling people by calling them names because you never know when you might call someone a scoundrel on the same day he's searching for his true identity. Who knows, Charles Manson may have considered himself quite the lady's man till he heard someone call him Jack the Ripper.

These excessive nosebleeds, which he has every six months or so, may be undoing all the progress I thought we'd made to make him a more stoic human being. He's never been shy about showing his blood. I have tried to tell him before that the more hurt he endures the less painful it becomes, but I think he's taken this the wrong way. I think he's chosen abundance over endurance. When I say his blood is everywhere I mean it's painted across his hands and face, smeared along the countertop, splashed beneath the faucet where it has pooled and splattered in the wash basin.

His hips slide sideways as if he has become woozy, as if he has lost his balance, but then he catches himself. I suspect he's waiting to hear what I have to say, if I have anything to say at all. Suddenly I remember I have left the car warming outside. "Don't go anywhere," I tell him, then I head downstairs.

My son is not tall for his age and I often think he's younger than he truly is. He is not just leaning over the sink pitched upon his elbows, he is teetering over the edge of self-reliance, of independence, and of growing up...on the verge of not being a boy anymore and not needing his old man for times like these. Sometimes it's hard to see the parts that we'll be missing when they're still with us, but both sides to this moment still seem easy to see. For now, for today, he is still a boy and his old man doesn't know how to stop the bleeding.

It's November. For the first time this fall the car is wrapped in a white skin that is frozen and gleaming in the hard cold air, sparkling like a vampire in the Twilight movies. The windows are gray with ice. Up above, bleached clouds stain a wide open sky. The blue of it ripples at the edges where trees shake their branches, battling the wind. I turn the motor off and walk back inside.

He is still standing over the sink, his nose still dripping. But at least it's dripping and not running. If it was running I would have to do something about it, something more extreme, even though I don't know what that is. I stop myself from telling him to tilt his head back, which would be to repeat a mistake I've made before. It's not good enough to tell him to plug his nose with toilet tissue as I did when I was a kid, for this is the age of the internet and he has told me numerous times that the ways that once worked for me just don't work anymore...as if my beliefs are as outmoded as screaming villagers bearing hunting torches. As if I'd once slaughtered goats or thrown virgins into seething volcanoes. As if my sacrifices weren't always designed by accident. I have no choice but to stand by, to watch his blood run down the drain because that's what the internet says I should do, and who can argue with the internet?

What the internet seems to teach us is that there

is one right way for everything. It is not a place for compromise but a place that strives to make all things black or white. But we need those gray areas for when we fall short. For love. The internet can be a cruel place to settle arguments, for nothing in our lives ever seems quite that absolute. When we hit a wall we need to believe that somewhere there still lies a viable alternative, for better or for worse.

I look up nosebleeds on my phone and I make sure he sees me reading about the appropriate thing to do. I tell him I'm reading directly from the text: "It says here to pinch your nose."

"I am," he says, showing annoyance, looking at me as if I can't see him. So I go on as if I can't.

"It says to slide your fingers down the bridge of your nose to a point just below the hard edge of bone, well before your nostrils. Pinch right there where it starts to get bendable, where there's cartilage." My son believes in numbers as much as he believes in anything. "It works 94% of the time," I tell him. He does as I say and the drops of blood rain down faster than they did before. The internet said not to tilt the head back or to stuff the nose with TP, but I don't tell him that because that he already knows. Instead I recite words like 'anterior' and 'septum,' words I would never use on my own, to give my voice the sound of authority. I mention words like 'cauterize' and 'embolization' because I know he will look them up and become less prone to letting his nose bleed more than is absolutely necessary the next time, which will most likely be about six months from now, and I can't help but wonder whether or not he will still be with me. "Turn the water on," I tell him. "And while you're standing there clean up the sink."

He does this with one hand while continuing to hold his nose with the other. I wipe down the counter and toss the spent tissue into the toilet which now looks like a cauldron of blood. Inside the sink a series of red circles, the dried outer edges of blood spatter, remain like chalk on pavement where dead bodies once were strewn. I'm about to tell him he must not be doing it right when I notice his nose has quit dripping.

"Stay there," I say, "and don't move."

Even though the internet said it wouldn't do any good I hurry downstairs to crush some ice and wrap it in a damp wash cloth. When I pass this to him he accepts it so readily, with such grace and obvious gratitude, that I feel my breath falter with emotion. "Go lie down," I tell him. "In bed, and take your shoes off." He knows this will make him late for school but he does what he is told. Not once has he mentioned calling his mother and I don't know if it's right to feel grateful for this or not.

Just last night, when I was feeling like a horrible parent for mishandling a situation where I caught him cheating at cards, afterward when he was upstairs sulking alone in his room and I was downstairs licking my self-inflicted wounds in the dark, I texted him. I told him that I used to think I was good at everything. I told him I once thought I was a good husband, a grateful son and an encouraging, loving father, but now I knew I was wrong. His mother says I tell him too much, that I shouldn't talk to him like I do, as if he was an adult--as if he wasn't a human being. For years she told me that I didn't talk to her enough. What I've since realized but still haven't told her is that our son already knows that I am better at helping others than I am at helping myself. He already knows if anyone can help me it's him. In the text I also told him that I loved him, that

I always would no matter what happened next, both because I knew it needed to be said and because I knew it to be true.

Why is it so hard to talk to our kids without pretending we're someone else, as if it wasn't us who made the same mistakes our kids are making? Why do our children seem so often to hate us when we are so willing to love them anyway? Why does this not work with our husbands and wives?

I have not been able to reconcile my divorce any better than my son has. The best I've been able to come up with in the past five years is that his mother and I married because we each had essential things that we needed to say to another, to show someone significant that life was what we thought it should be, to say those things that we ourselves had longed to hear. She told me that she loved me and would love me forever, but as soon as she said it I knew it wasn't true. I had been taught to believe that actions spoke louder than words but I just wasn't watching. I had thought that even if our marriage paled in comparison to our rosy expectations we'd end up a shade closer to where we wanted to be. But now I'm not so sure. She's moved on to the next thing, the next man, while I'm still trying to figure out what happened to her last one.

Now, this morning, I find myself lying next to my son on his bed, wondering if the blood he spilled in the sink originally belonged to his mother or to me. I want to tell him that the older we get the more we realize the best parts of our lives are not what we do alone, that what we remember is what we do with others, but I don't know if he's old enough to hear this or not. I don't even know if the life I'm living is my own. Nothing that happens seems to stay. My thoughts and experiences seem as fleeting as snow, not sticking long enough for anything else to hold on to. But I can't help it--I keep going after what's already gone, as if that in itself could make it stay. I keep tripping on past moments that rise up like bumps in a rug, like ripples in the sky.

The house is still and quiet. The sound of the radio only now becomes apparent. Music rises up the stairs like smoke from the kitchen. Like a memory in soft shoes. Warm and sentimental. Feeling tidal within the pulse of my blood. Is it Jackson Browne? Or perhaps The Four Seasons? I can't quite remember. I can't reach back far enough to know. There seems to be something unfamiliar in the music, as if I just haven't listened to it carefully enough before. Is that the sound of a steel guitar?

O-oh won't you stay-ay-ay
Just a little bit long-ger?
Please, please, please
Say-ay you-ou wi-i-i-illll...

I know I don't need to. I know his bloody nose is all but over, but still, I tell him to give it time, that sometimes there's nothing to do but wait, and the hours pass most quickly when we're asleep.

Researchers at Northwestern University now say memories have the power to heal themselves, unlike the scars that get buried intractably in our skin. They tell us the more we revisit our memories the more we rewrite them and the less they resemble what actually happened. I look around my son's room, wondering how we'll remember this differently. His bent right leg leans against my hip. The wash cloth with the ice rests on his chest unused and all but melted. A large wet mark reaches up and disappears under his chin. It spreads down and across his body as if his heart is melting. He's been living with me for less than a year. His room is not only a mess, which can be expected, but his closet remains empty. Among the piles of clothing and scattered potato chip bags that litter the floor there are video game boxes, his laptop and iPod and eBook. Two stacks of framed pictures not yet hung still lean against the walls, and there is a shelf his mother bought for him in order to organize his belongings that remains in its original box, not yet opened.

When my son first arrived from his mother's to live with me for the first time in five years he was jealous if not outright scorned by how well I treated my dog. Now he calls to me, to look at the two of them sitting side by side. Now she lies on her back so comfortably beside him that she falls asleep and does not awaken when he plays with her paws. He keeps asking me to look at them, and he keeps breaking my heart.

His mother tells me that since our divorce she's learned how to forgive. I don't tell her that since our divorce I've forgotten how. To forgive is to accept things as they were, as they are and as they will be...to give them permission to stay or to go. I can see no good that could come from accepting what a senseless act divorce can be. Regardless of fault, even under the best circumstances, the edge that continues to cut separates us from half the life we could have had with our children.

Earlier this morning when my son was brushing his teeth and laying his hair down for school, before the nosebleed, I found him making faces at himself in the mirror. When he looked at me but kept making the faces it made me uncomfortable. But since then I've come to think that he must have been practicing how to look at girls. He doesn't know yet that it's best to just leave these faces behind. He doesn't know any better than I did that what we're supposed to show is what lies inside. Now, looking over at my son, he seems to be asleep so I get up as quietly as I can, trying not to disturb him.

"Where do you think you're going?" he says.

But I don't know where I'm going. His voice is just a whisper and when I hear it I have to wonder if this is something I've asked myself. It seems all I've ever done is leave.

"Stay," he says. Then in a voice so clean and pure, so white as snow, he talks to me.

HUNTING MRS. ELJINHOLMES'

My father would not have dinner with the rest of his family when he had things on his mind. He would go into the living room to eat by himself. There in the dark he would sit in his rocker beside the fire. No one could be with him but his dog.

One such night when the house was filling with cold and a winter wind was pulsing against the windows, when the small sounds of us eating were overrun by the sound of Uncle Jim chasing my father's fork across his plate, frozen rain began pelting the roof.

"Yeste'dy Uncle Jim said we was gonna get rain," my father called. His spirit had risen and my mother smiled. Her shoulders softened under the full sound of my father's voice. When Jim's tail bent a certain way my father claimed it was a sure sign it was going to rain. Uncle Jim was my father's dog and had been with my father longer than anyone in our family, including my mother. He said Jim was almost human, though we knew he got along best with him because he wasn't.

I think Jim represented to my father a part of his younger self, a part that he liked, the larger, rougher and happier part that got lost in the accident. He used Jim to communicate with us when otherwise he didn't know how. My father was once a faller for Crown but was filling in as a choker setter. He was busting his tail to keep the logs moving when the haul back line snapped and the cable tried to cut him in two.

My father's rocking chair moaned as he pulled and pushed and wrestled himself to his feet. His injury had broken something irreplaceable inside him. I listened to the thump of his wooden leg as he came toward us in the kitchen. This was my father's second wooden leg, the one he carved from vine maple. His first came from the spruce that nearly killed him, which he'd carved out of spite. One day the leg broke as if to add insult to injury and it sent him again cart wheeling to the ground. We sat with him to watch it burn.

As I was eating he put his hand on my shoulder. "Hunt with us in the mornin?" Hunting had been something I enjoyed.

The rain had drawn my father out of the stupor in which he had fallen. His talking was a sure sign of that. And he was talking clearly. Mostly my father talked inside his mouth, as if he had no teeth, as if it was more important for him to speak than to be heard. He did not like to repeat himself, so when he spoke we all listened carefully.

"Jim found an orchard way up back the old place. We should be all right." By which he meant that it was a secluded place where we would not get caught hunting. Other than Jim I was the only one my father took hunting. I was twelve, the youngest and the only one who could not remember my father ever having two legs.

We never hunted exclusively for sport in our

family. We hunted for food, in and out of season. My father had been waiting for rain so we could go. In the morning, just before light, the rain-softened leaves helped to hide his clumsy steps.

We passed through a stand of alder to get to the orchard. Despite the rain the woods were filled with light. There were not many leaves on the trees and the rain fell easily between the bare limbs and it splashed noisily on the ground. Thick bracken, vine maple and salal filled the gaps in the dark timber that grew against the hills. In this we hid ourselves. While my father scanned the trails below us I rolled myself into a ball and fell asleep.

At the time of my father's accident, between the time the log got stumped and the point when the cable broke he said he heard a voice cry "JUMP!" and without thinking he did what the voice told him to do, just before the haul-back line cracked, broke and whipped. The cable lashed into his legs. Had he not jumped when the voice told him to he would have been cut in half at the waist. As it was, he lost his right leg just above the knee.

He could not say where the voice came from yet he knew it was the voice of his grandmother. "Later," he once told me, "if I can…I'll come back to watch over you."

Curled up there, near the orchard, I felt my father grab my leg. He squeezed until I woke. He and Jim were looking down at me. My father held a finger over his lips. I shrugged my shoulders. He pointed at something in the brush that I could not find. Despite everything he'd taught me he took a chance and fired one shot.

Our eyes spotted no movement. There was no sound of rustling brush. We moved anxiously to the spot. When we got there my father's head dropped low on his shoulders. He cussed inside his mouth. The deer was too small. By my father's own standards it was a waste of life. "We don't leave'em," he said.

He was ashamed enough by what he'd done that he would not allow me to watch him gut the animal. He even pushed Jim away. While my father dressed the deer, Jim and I sat watching the woods. We listened to the sound of my father's hands, feeling their way through the wet body, separating the deer from its warm insides.

You know my father was a man of few words. Through his actions and his hard, reproachful looks, he tried to teach common sense to me and my two brothers. He said if we had common sense we would be able to teach ourselves anything. He told us sooner or later we all become victims of ourselves, that only common sense would determine how long it took.

When leaving the woods my father made me go ahead. I think he did not want my eyes upon him. I carried his gun while he carried the deer.

The day should have been over. The hunting, the waiting, the walking had been enough. But then, so suddenly, as if they had dropped from the trees, two dogs attacked Jim. Both were German shepherds, one much larger than the other. Jim didn't have a chance. They had him down on his back.

My father dropped the deer and ran hobbling to save Jim. The dogs bit him on the hands when he tried to break them up. He tried using his wooden leg, but it was awkward and he lost his balance. He fell down and from his back he jabbed his leg again and again into the dogs. The woods were filled with the sound of animals tearing at one another. The small shepherd backed away when the larger one got a tight hold on Jim's chest. He began to shake him. My father withdrew his knife and crawled to where Jim was suffering. He beat on the shepherd's head with the handle end, but the dog would not let go. Jim began to howl desperately. That's when my father turned the knife around and stabbed into the big dog's shoulder.

Both shepherds ran off, the larger one limping and coughing. Jim remained on the ground, lying on his side, barking and growling as if the fight was still going on.

"Good boy," my father said, now lying on the ground, curled around Jim. He stroked Jim carefully, soothing and quieting him. "Good boy." He kept talking calmly to his dog. Tears began to surface in his eyes. I think he tried not to disturb Jim because he knew he was dying. He leaned over his dog, stroking and soothing with his chapped and bloodied hands until he was sure Jim's breathing had stopped. Then, for the first and only time, I saw my father give way to his insides. He began to cry, almost silently. He began to choke, and the crying shook his body.

I offered to carry the deer but he shook his head to turn me down. He could not carry both, although for awhile he tried, so he decided to bury Jim there in the woods. He wrapped the dog in his coat. He placed his hat and his knife in the hole, on top of Jim's body. Then he slowly pushed the dirt in with his hands. I sat away from them, beneath the heavy sway of a cedar bough.

Before he could finish, the smaller shepherd returned. She stood twenty feet away, pointing, growling quietly. She began very slowly to approach my father, one step at a time, as if she thought she was invisible. Then she stopped. She held one leg tensely off the ground but would close no further. My father stood up. He reached for his rifle. As he put the gun to his shoulder a voice went off in my head.

But my father did not hear the voice. I think he chose not to. He chose to pull the trigger instead. A second shot came so close behind the first that it splintered the sound, and the two echoes became one. The second shot stung my father in the chest. He looked at me, not understanding what happened. He looked confused but not frightened. He stared at me, and his breathing became strained. His eyes began to close. He looked at the shepherd lying small against the ground. It was still wheezing and puffing. My father's face filled with anguish. He swallowed once, very hard. Then his life left him. And his body twisted as it fell.

I searched the woods with my eyes, hunkered down low, listening carefully through the rain, waiting for my father's voice to sound inside my head.

WHAT TO KNOW
ABOUT THE WATER

I'm on the beach with my brother's wife. She's sitting small and dark in the seat beside me. It's me who's behind the wheel. She's had a few driving lessons from my brother, but she's suspicious now of everything he's ever told her. It seems impossible that they will ever learn anything positive from one another. She's twenty-eight and rarely leaves the house. Their two kids are asleep in the back seat, piled on top of one another like two hands gripped together. Behind the kids, behind their seat, wrapped in a sandy blanket is a harbor seal pup. Its large black eyes match those of the children. We're on our way to the aquarium. I'm driving at normal speed over wet sand, aimed south between the soft dunes and the ocean, excited at the possibility of doing something good.

They aren't getting along, my brother and his wife. At best, this is what they do, get along. When not at their best, it's best they not be together. I don't know much about their relationship. At least I didn't. I didn't want to know. Until today.

My brother's wife is Filipino, but what I have

to say is not about Filipinos. What I have to say is about her. What I'm not saying is that the fault with their marriage is hers because she's different from my brother. Not as blonde or white or whatever. What I am saying is that their differences are large, that this makes communication difficult.

I'm not going to use their names, my brother's and his wife's. I'll say his and hers and you'll know who I'm talking about.

He says he doesn't let things bother him. Largely, I think this is true. He seems to have an infinite capacity for denial.

Consequently he has become a compulsive liar, a bankrupt, a horse trader and a petty thief. I have often thought of him as the Last of the North American Pirates. In this lies his greatness, the source of his life's adventure. He is, however, a marvelously loving father. All I'm saying about my brother is what I'd say about everyone I know: He wants the best for his own but has no real idea how to get it. Nor does he know when he has it. All he seems to know is that he will sacrifice everything for his kids, including his wife. He's traded her love before.

When we first got into the car she said she did not want to talk. Fine with me. I said we'd go to the beach, look at the water. Maybe feel the healing effect of open spaces. On the way there she began to talk about my brother. Openly. Without regard for the kids. I shushed her with one finger over my lips. I pointed a thumb at the kids. Every so often she would show her exasperation by jerking her knotted fingers out of her lap. Then she would throw them back down against her thighs.

To cross the language barrier we use a lot of hand gestures instead of words. Maybe they should use fewer words and more of their bodies, my brother and his wife. Maybe not. She is a small woman, and it seems at this moment that it is her anger and not her stature that keeps her feet from touching the floor. She looks to be holding her breath as she contends with some inner conflict that might levitate her, that might free her from her present life. She says she does not know what to do, and she shakes her head, and the roundness of her mouth rolls carefully over each letter of every word, as if her tongue can sense the sharpness there.

Before we got to the beach, which was only a ten-minute drive, the kids had fallen fast to sleep. If I weren't driving I'd be asleep, too. I've always slept best in a traveling car. It has to do with the womb, I think. The moving and the rocking, the trusting that you're under someone else's care.

Before we found the seal pup, after the kids fell asleep, I learned about the courtship of my brother and his wife. About their written correspondence. About all the perfect pictures used to close the marriage deal. We drove slowly with the windows down, watching the water.

They were married in the Philippines. At the time my brother had a steady mill job here. A laborer's job that has since gone by the wayside. The company was bought up by another and when they rehired they chose not to take back the pirates and the petty thieves. They had a big wedding, as usual. A big celebration. Like we do. My brother has told me, and his wife has confirmed, that when a man marries a Filipino woman he marries her family as well. Which means he supports them financially.

I admit I've become more interested in them now that I've seen what a tough time they're having. I've been watching this for a long time in different people, different couples. I stand gaping at our ability to accept what we know will ultimately do us harm. When I prompt my brother's wife for details I'm asking for the facts as she knows them. I will accept her version of the truth. My brother would never give one up. I ask her not to tell me anything she has not already told my brother. I figure then I won't have to be on one side or the other. I hope to keep at a safe place somewhere in the middle, in the stuff that they both know about. I'm not a confidante. I'm not a judge. I won't be swayed to one side or the other. I'm only a hole in the ground. All I do if I do anything is repeat back as honestly as I can what it is she's told me.

They have money trouble. Who doesn't? This seems to be at the heart of every argument. He overextends their credit, and for this she calls him irresponsible and even stupid. I asked her, to his face you call him stupid? She admits she does. She insists that it is stupid. I cannot argue. But still, it is this that I was talking about earlier, the subtleties of language that get lost in the cracks between different cultures. She has not always wanted to insult him. Reason is what she was after, communication. But she hurts him instead. My brother says he does not feel pain.

It isn't just the money, she claims. It's the lying, the things he does to cover up the reckless outpouring of money. The glove box in the car, for example, where she found all the unopened bills. And the broken promises about life in America. How easy. How happy. How complete. Like kings and queens. She says she left a lover in the Philippines to come here, to marry my brother to help her family. She says she helps her family but she cannot pay her own bills, she cannot help herself. She says she knows why my brother had to go to the Philippines for a wife. Because no one here would have him. She criticizes him, his lying, his poor money handling, his clothes. And now, more recently, his belly, and even his penis. You've told him all this? *Yes*. Openly? *Yes*. And he criticized her back, in kind, openly, for watching TV, for sleeping all the time, for lack of interest in sex, for fear of things that haven't happened yet. *I have to be honest, don't I?* She says.

She says she would leave him but she cannot leave the kids. I never used to understand that. I thought parents believed a nasty home was better than a split family, for the sake of the kids. But that's not it. Parents can't live without their kids. It's more about the parents' need for the children than the other way around. We'd rather let our spouses slowly kill us than willingly leave our children.

Why is there such a fine line between being honest and being cruel? Why do we try to know more than we are experiencing at any given moment? Why do we eat our own hearts then blame others when we find them missing?

She tells me about her first night spent in the U.S. How her flight to Portland got delayed in San Francisco. How afraid she was to be alone, my brother waiting for her at the Portland airport. How her English became no good after she became afraid. How the airline took her to an expensive hotel even after she told them all she had was five dollars. They just smiled back at this woman who would not quit waving the $5 bill. She did not understand the room was free. She did not understand the plastic card they gave to her was the key to enter the room. So she waited outside room 211, the number now frozen in her mind, for over an hour until a bellhop helped her to get inside. Then she was afraid to use the toilet, and she slept on the floor, because she thought she might not have to pay for the room if she used none of its amenities. An expensive hotel in San Francisco, gotten to via a piece of paper and a shuttle from the airport. She did not eat, so not to use the only money she had. My brother sent her $200 for the flight over, for situations just like this. But she gave to her family all but $5 upon her departure from Manila. Innocent new queen of America.

We had reached another point of silence, my brother's wife and I. She had let out her story, her anger, pain and frustration, and I had told her what she said. I had suggested that she and my brother, if they did not want to continue like this, would have to come together or separate. I told her nothing but I said it plainly. And in that raging silence, driving down the open beach, the kids asleep and she all full of that topsy-turvy thoughtfulness, I spotted the seal pup glistening in the summer sun, lying at the water's edge, a red gash on its round rubbery head.

It's common knowledge among those who live here that we are not to touch seal pups that are abandoned on the beach. I know this. I know the mother seals are out running errands, rounding up dinner but will return. I know that mother seals often do not reclaim their pups if they smell the touch of man. What I did not know was what to do if confronted by a pup that was wounded. It could have been struck by a propeller, I thought, or it could have been hit with a club by one of our angry fishermen. I knew of an aquarium nearby that kept seals, so we corralled the guy onto a blanket without touching him. We put him in the back of the car and headed south along the beach.

Seeing her laughing, my brother's wife, as we carefully captured this lost child of a wild animal, seeing her full of nervous fear and joy I thought, yes, you must get out. You must get my brother and the kids and bust out to the beach, to the lake, to the woods. Look hard and long out over the Pacific water and see if you can truly see the home you have and the home you left. Forget all this nonsense that comes from wherever it comes from, from being locked in a house all the time, from watching TV, sleeping, being afraid of America. Where it comes from does not matter. Getting through it does.

But we were still not talking. Not about America. Not about my brother or his problems or the Philippines. Not even about the seal pup. We looked back at the kids and watched them sleep. We knew they must see the pup before we let it go. We did not yet know that the people at the aquarium would rebuke us for our efforts then turn us down. We did not know we would spend an hour in a parking lot waiting for the different law enforcement agencies to decide who had to handle this one. We did not know the sheriff would escort us back to the beach to return the injured pup to the sand. We felt we had no way of knowing that the mother could inflict these wounds herself.

Some of us are just fools with broken hearts and perhaps that is all we'll ever be. If by chance we find one of those who can know and love and accept us for who we are they may forgive the recurrence of our same mistakes. I assume this could be true though I have never seen it. The only way to know is to quit or to keep on looking.

After releasing the pup, I returned to the passenger side of the car. The kids were awake and the sheriff was keeping an eye on the young seal. I told my brother's wife I refused to drive anymore. I told her I was going to sleep and she could drive along the beach, or anywhere she wanted. I assured her that by the time we left the beach she would know how to drive like an American. That she must trust her instincts when her knowledge failed. That she could go wherever she wanted, and I only asked that she not wake me till we got there. I showed her the two pedals on the floor, the gear shift, and I told her to stay on the hard sand away from the water and the soft dunes. I even told her she could follow our tracks back home. I told her all she needed to know. The rest, I said, is up to you.

BLACKBIRD

The phone was ringing. When the kid thought it wouldn't quit he picked it up. His voice was changing. Not even his mother could tell him apart from his dad now. Some lady started talking to him like she knew who he was. He heard some of what the lady was trying to say, how cut up she was about some dog. That's when he told her he wasn't his dad. She said her name was Meryl. The kid told her to hang on. Outside, down the driveway, his dad was up to his waist under his mom's car, both hands covered in grease. The car was bruised and dented and reddish purple like a heart. It belonged to the boy's mother who'd left it behind when she left his dad. His dad was finally trying to get the damned thing working. He said he was going to sell it but before it could move it needed to run. The kid told him some Meryl was on the phone to talk about some dog. First the man said, "Who?" Then when he realized he didn't know who Meryl was he knew why she was calling. "Son-of-a-bitch," he said. Then he dropped his tools on the ground and drug himself out from under the car.

"You feel like going for a ride? You maybe

could learn something," the man said.

They'd been walking on eggshells all morning, till the phone rang, then the man was dead set on taking the boy along, so he could teach the boy something, something he knew the boy knew nothing about. So the boy said, "Sure, I'll go for a ride," and the boy didn't ask where they were going.

By the time the man put the phone down in its cradle to go to his room he wasn't angry anymore. The boy thought he must be changing his clothes but when he came back he looked the same. Not even his arms or his hands had been washed.

"You going like that?" The boy said.

"You sound like your mother," the man said.

"That's funny," the boy said. "Mom said I sound like you. A lot of people say I sound like you." But the man didn't say anything. "So where we going?"

"Have a job to do."

"What kind of job?"

"Gotta take care of a dog."

For his truck to leave the driveway the man had to manage his way around his wife's car. Gradually the road was widening beside the car and the truck's tire tracks were cutting through the grass and into the dirt. The boy thought they were going to feed the dog or something, like the owner was out of town. But when they got there a woman was standing on the porch waiting with her arms folded. Though the boy already knew who the woman was the man told him her name was Meryl. Meryl handed the man a foil package that fit perfectly into the palm of his hand. By the time the boy shook Meryl's hand her hand was cold.

"Just like you ask me for," she said. The man passed the foil to the boy. It felt too hot for the boy to hold but the boy thought if Meryl could hold it then so could he. He knew his dad had work-calloused hands but not Meryl. This made him think of his mom again who could wash dishes in scalding hot water with her bare hands. "She's over here," Meryl said, but she said it like she didn't want to. Her voice was a whisper. She led them around the corner outside the house. "I put her on the old blanket," Meryl said, before rounding the next corner. "Just like you ask me to." She looked at the man in a way that made the boy feel like he didn't know who she was talking to, like she knew she was asking something of his dad that the boy didn't know he had. Then single file they approached the dog on the blanket.

"What's her name?" the man said.

"Blackbird," Meryl said. The dog's ears moved like it was listening but its tail didn't budge. "Same as mine," she said. Then she kneeled on the wet ground in her clean white dress. She began petting the dog and saying her name.

"Why don't you introduce us," the man said to Meryl. So Meryl took his hand and laid it softly on the dog's head. Then Meryl started to choke. Her hand was still on the man's hand that was on the dog, like they were giving the dog a blessing. The boy didn't know if she was going to cry or get sick. Then the man had to ask, "Did you get the shovel?" Meryl nodded and took her hand off the man's hand and pointed over at a tree where the shovel was standing with its blade stuck in the ground. Then the dog began to whimper and Meryl rose to her feet. She was holding to the dog's back like she was trying to keep her balance, then she had to kneel back down again.

"One last time," she said. She held the dog's ears in her hands and kissed it on the head. Then she rose and walked quickly to the corner of her house leaning over like she wanted to run. The boy didn't know where she was going or what was happening.

The sky was white and the man was talking as he was petting the dog. His words were for his son but he was whispering for the dog. "You don't have to help if you don't want," he whispered. But still the boy didn't know what the man needed help with. After the argument they'd already had that morning about his not wanting to help with the car it wasn't right to quit on his dad again. "You don't have to be here no more," the man said. "Not if you don't want."

"I'm already here," the boy said, not knowing at all where he was.

"Come feed her then," the man said. He was still in the same place beside the dog so the boy kneeled down in front of her, right where Meryl had been. The dog's mouth was soft. She was eating like she wasn't hungry but the meatloaf was too good to refuse. She was being gentle. Her tongue was moving slow like her whole mouth was frozen. "Just a little at a time," the man said. "One big bite for last." Then he took a small bite for himself and let the dog lick his fingers. He had his other hand behind his back. The boy fed the dog her last bite. When she swallowed, the man brought his hand from behind his back and in his hand was a gun and he shot the dog in the ear. It happened fast, too fast for the boy to know what happened. The sound of the gun was ringing in the boy's head. He didn't know what to do and the man was looking him in the eye. "She was suffering," he explained. "Meryl couldn't take no more."

The man was looking at his boy, waiting for him to speak, but the boy was busy wondering if maybe

Meryl had been watching them through a window somewhere. He wondered if she could've heard them. He even wondered if she didn't see them but still heard them if she thought his and his father's voices were the same, so he tried to remember how they sounded and what they might have said.

"Son. This here is not a bad thing. If it was me this is how I'd have it go." But the boy saw the dog's mouth was crooked. She looked like she'd been broken into.

"Just don't be calling me when your time comes," the boy said. Then he said, "You said we were taking care of a dog. Not killing one."

Then a lot of things ran through the man's mind. He had a lot of things stored up that he could say, but instead he said, "First time's the hardest."

"I don't believe you. How's it supposed to get easier?"

"It don't," the man confessed. They tried to look at one another but they looked at the ground instead. "You can dig the hole over there by the shovel. Or you can watch or go wait in the truck." The man began to wrap the dog in the blanket. The boy left the foil on the ground when he walked away.

Not even when the boy slammed the truck's door did Meryl look to see if it was over. She knew it was better not to look at such things. The boy could still see what had happened.

When the man returned to the front of the house he leaned the shovel next to Meryl's door. That's when the boy first saw the blackbirds painted on the tops of Meryl's white shutters. Then the man pulled himself into the truck but he didn't like what he saw so he slipped out again to put the shovel in the garage instead. He took the ball of foil from his pocket and tossed it behind the seat. He pulled the driver's door closed without slamming it, then he took one last look at the house. In the mean time the boy figured out what he wanted to say. "Why did Meryl call you? I mean, why you?" he asked.

The man said lots of people called him. He didn't know why they thought of him when they needed this kind of help. "Probably because they think it'll hurt me less than it'll hurt them," he said. "And I guess word just gets around."

From inside the cab the boy had never seen such bright colors before, or such a variety of colors, new colors that made things look more alive. The black bench seat looked not worn but stained with purple. The trees were floating in the sky with the clouds. The water bathing in the light of the river. The rusted orange hood of the truck looked more like a traveling sunset than some rumbling metal thing. And the blue that made up the road ahead. He expected the asphalt would be black, or old and gray, but it was blue, pure, unsoiled. The stripes running down the sides of the road were more silver than white, like vapor trails streaking through a clear blue sky. They were on their way home, following the blue of the ground before them, while everything behind slowly drained, fading to black and white.

Meanwhile the woman's car was still blocking the driveway, like nothing in the world had changed. They passed it like it wasn't really there. The boy had been looking out the windows while thinking about talking to his mother, thinking about telling her all that he had seen, though he knew she wouldn't be home when he arrived. Even if she was, he thought she wouldn't hear him and perhaps never had.

PRIUS

They were only two now, father and son and no one else. The man was driving his boy to school, two trips to and from, each day every day. The last stretch of gray road leading to the school reminded him of the roads at home that bled out into the country. He'd not driven this road for any reason other than to reach the school. The boy was in the latter part of his first year in high school. The morning was like any other morning except it was May, the sun was up and it was already warm. Then, up ahead in the other lane, it looked like a road kill coming up, a bird or a cat or something. The man turned his head. He'd seen all he wanted to see of that sort of thing. The morning rush was on yet everyone slowed their cars to edge carefully around whatever it was there in the road.

"You see that chicken?" the boy said. "There was a chicken back there sitting in the road." The man looked quickly into his side view mirror. Sure enough, some bird was holding its head up, just watching the traffic go by. It was definitely alive.

"Son of a gun," the man said. "A chicken. Crossing the road. Now I've seen everything."

"What was the chicken doing sitting in the road?"

"It was just sitting there," the man said.

"No, it's a joke. Why was the chicken sitting in the road?"

"I don't know," the man said. "Tell me."

"Make a guess, come on. What was the chicken doing sitting in the road?"

"I don't know. Changing its mind?"

"Changing its mind?"

"You know. It goes, Why did the chicken cross the road? But it was just sitting there, so it must have changed its mind. About crossing the road." The man was looking at the road, then he looked back to his son. "So you going to tell me or what?" But now the boy was watching the road, too. "Well are you?"

"No. Your answer was better than mine."

It was only another minute to school. The boy was trying to think of a better punch line while the man was thinking about the real chicken sitting in the road. How he should have stopped to save it from getting run over.

Before getting out the boy said, "There's nothing funny about a chicken crossing the road when it's a real live chicken."

"I'm going back for it," the man said. Then before his son got out of earshot he said, "Hey! If it doesn't go well for the chicken...how about the three of us get together for dinner? How's that sound?"

The boy came back to the car window. He didn't want to yell. He felt like he was still too new at school to yell. "Really, Dad? Road kill for dinner? That's a new low on the dinner menu, even for you, Dad." Then the boy patted the palm of his hand on the roof of the car and he was gone.

The new low on the menu would be how the

man felt if he found the chicken dead in the road. Everyone was in a rush to get someplace else at that time in the morning. He started to give himself excuses for why he hadn't stopped, like how his son would have been late to school if he'd stopped for the chicken. Then he told himself he couldn't have stopped anyway, because there were too many cars behind him. And besides that, it didn't make sense to stop by the time he recognized what it was. He'd had to look far back through his side view mirror and by that time he was too far down the road. There was nothing he could have done before now and now he was going to stop while he was on the right side of the road. When he neared the spot where the chicken had been there was a sky blue Prius sitting on the shoulder of the road with its flashers on. The chicken was nowhere in sight.

The driver of the Prius was inside the car. She hadn't had time to walk it back into the grass, so she must have put it inside the car with her, most likely still alive. That's all the man could make of it. It's not what he would have done. He would have taken the chicken back into the grass and laid it down, perhaps after making it a nest. In all the 'chicken crossing the road' stories no one ever said where the chickens came from.

Now the left flasher was the only one going on the Prius so the man slowed to a full stop and waved her on. A hand quickly shot out the driver's window but it was too fast to see if the driver was a man or a woman. He assumed it would be a woman. He couldn't know how long the chicken had been in the road but no one else had stopped so the woman must be like one in a million. The man asked himself, Why was the chicken sitting in the road? So he could find the woman in the sky blue Prius.

So now he was after the blue Prius. At the first intersection the left blinker went on again. The traffic light was already yellow but she was going for it. As the car turned broadside to him he saw it was indeed a woman driving. Then he ran the red light. When he'd thought about saving the chicken he thought he'd have to let it scratch or peck at him in order to pick it up. He wondered if the woman had gotten pecked or scratched. He had decided he would just let nature take its course after putting the chicken back in the grass, but the woman thought differently. She was taking the chicken someplace. That now seemed like the better thing to do. He thought she must be a better person than he was.

The Prius seemed to be going pretty fast, but then at this time in the morning everyone was going a little faster than usual. Everyone had some place else to be. He wanted to know how the woman was different from him. He wanted to know how she decided to take the chicken with her. Of course it would make sense that she was headed to a veterinarian. That would make the most sense of all, if the chicken was injured. But the Prius had now gone through the last light in town. It was headed straight out into the country. Her chance to get the bird to an emergency veterinarian had passed. Where on earth was she going with that chicken? Then the man laughed. He thought perhaps it was her chicken and she'd been tracking its escape for days.

She was on a straight stretch and picking up speed. He didn't want to lose her. Then the thought occurred to him that she might be a veterinarian herself. He wanted to apologize to her for something, for everything, and for passing the chicken in the first place. But he wouldn't tell her his plan had been only to put the chicken back in the grass. He couldn't tell her that, not right away. He would tell her that part later. First he would apologize for following her, though that seemed a horrible way to start a conversation, unless he wanted her to believe he was some kind of stalker. Only then did it occur to him that he didn't even know for sure that she had the chicken. Not for sure. Someone else could have gotten there before her. She could have only stopped to talk on her cell phone. She might not be a veterinarian, at all.

Of course she had the chicken, he thought. She had to have the chicken. And he would commend her for it--that's what he would do first. He would pull up to her window without getting out of his car and he would tell her what a good person she was for saving that chicken. Then he would confess everything to her because she was obviously that kind of person, a kind and gentle and forgiving person. He would confess all the bad things he had done before moving here, all that he could remember. There was so much he needed to say to her, if only she would stop and listen. So they could talk. Just the two of them. Perhaps then someone would know what was still good in him.

ZUCCHINI

It was the fifth of July and a group of neighborhood kids gathered together with what remained of their fireworks, both ground and aerial varieties, from sparklers and firecrackers to screaming bottle rockets and fiery Roman candles. They were beginning to light them off from the gravel of the dead end road. The man's son who was visiting from the coast was thirteen. Everyone agreed that he should be the one lighting the fuses because he was the oldest child there. Some parents were watching from inside their houses. The young couple from across the road was outside, sitting in their lawn chairs. The husband was drinking vodka and the wife was holding their only child while the sunset melted down to an orange and yellow ribbon that stretched across the horizon making the hills turn black and dusty.

The couple seated outside were imagining a time when their own child might be old enough to join such a group, but they were primarily out in front of their house to stand watch, to make sure the kids did not set fire to the dry limbs of the tall spruce that hanged out over the roof of the first home they might ever own. The woman said something to her husband so he got up and walked to the backyard. When he returned he carried a piece of plywood that he dropped on the road so the kids had a level place on which to stand their fireworks.

The 13-year-old's father had gone outside to collect his mail when he stopped in the middle of the road to watch the kids laughing and running and hiding behind one another. The woman and her husband beneath the dusty green hood of the blue spruce had become flickering images in the darkness, reflecting the changing light from the fireworks. The woman was still holding their 2-year-old son. The father was still seated on a low folding lawn chair that rested squarely on the ground beside his wife. Earlier that summer they'd had a tree trimming service come in to clear the first 20 feet of the tree trunk of its branches in order to bring more light into the house. Their neighbor, the one now standing in the road, had watched from inside his house knowing that if it were him he would have limbed the tree himself.

He had talked only once to the neighbor woman, at the row of mailboxes. She had told him her and her husband's names but he immediately forgot them. She was often home alone with her child but the man knew better than to visit with her while her husband was at work. There was only that one time when she told him that her sister's boyfriend had left his motorcycle with them when the couple broke up, that the woman and her husband now had the motorbike in their gardening shed and it took up too much room. She told him the motorcycle had fallen out of the back of a truck but otherwise it was fine and he could have it. That night her husband wheeled it over to the man's driveway for him to store inside his own garage. Months later when winter was over and the man was cleaning out his garage he rolled the motorcycle back out onto his driveway, but by next morning it was gone. Stolen. Which was fine by him because the couple had not followed through by bringing him the title as they said they would. So each time the man crossed the road to get his mail he did so after dark or when his neighbors were not working in their garden.

The man had his own garden, but it was behind the house that he rented that was surrounded by a tall wooden fence where no one could see. He had flowers. Gladiolus, Dahlias, China Pinks, Creeping Zinnias, and he had tall wide-faced sunflowers, the Russian Mammoth and the California Greystripe, flowers that he'd never grown before because the coastal climate that he was familiar with just wasn't dry enough to produce them. Of course he had the obligatory radishes and carrots that grew easily, and green peas that climbed all over the place, even a line of Jack-be-Little pumpkins that strayed out of the garden plot and into his lawn. A variety of small cherry tomato plants started popping up sponta-neously between the rows. There were red ones, yellow ones, and purple ones that really didn't look right enough to eat. Then there were pear shaped ones, also yellow, and these were all risen from the seeds of the fallen fruit from the prior tenant's gar-den the year before. But there were only two things in particular that the man really needed to grow, arti-chokes and marionberries. He had both the Globe and the Jerusalem varieties, and two thick rows of the long purple marions grown from cuttings he'd brought with him from the coast, lined up east to west for maximum exposure to the sun.

There was no reason for him to have artichokes

other than he liked to eat them, but his desire to grow marionberries had come from a family tradition where his grandmother had a roadside jam and jelly stand located on the family homestead. Not exactly a Walter Knott Berry Farm enterprise but it was good enough for them. In fact, Walter Knott had written to his grandmother a short but very polite letter when he heard about her berry stand. He'd invited the family down to see what he'd done with his berry farm, but the homestead family just wasn't the travelling kind, not since they landed in their own valley with all the timber and water they could ever want, after emigrating from Norway.

On the sheet of worn plywood placed on the ground in the middle of the gravel road the four younger boys were jumping as if they were trying to escape their own skin, as if they too could launch into the dark night sky from this level wooden platform. The woman seated across the road stood up, staring at the man standing alone in the road. She couldn't believe what her body was telling her. She was shocked to feel her personal convictions being tested, like leaves so easily shaken. She looked into the road again at the man standing in the darkness watching the children and she enjoyed a few carefree minutes to look at him while he wasn't looking at her, but then she felt as miserable as a flea running against the grain of all she'd ever loved, of all she thought she was. In her mind she could see his hands and the fine golden hairs and she could feel them passing beneath her clothes, brushing against the skin of her soft arms and legs. She could feel the touch and the powdery cool scrub of his chest against hers. She was hot and wet and her skin was flushed. The heat was rising through her, trying to break free. It started in her stomach then ran to her chest and lower back before it turned into a wash of heat that wound and roped its way through the muscles of her back and shoulders, ending in a liquid that produced a small drowning sweat that rose from her lower back again, like a flood following the track of her spine to crest on the back of her neck and shoulders.

Each clash of powder and spark sent a splash of lightening quick shadows pulsing across the garden, staying low to the ground beside the small blue house. Her husband now saw the man standing in the road. He held up his bottle as a greeting. "Happy fifth of July!" he laughed, inviting the man over for a drink. The man waved one of his berry-stained hands saying first he had to run inside. When he returned he brought with him a half pint of marionberry jelly that he'd canned just that morning. The woman remained standing and her husband directed the man to sit in his place but the woman was trying to remove herself so she stood up instead. Then her husband stood to go inside to retrieve another glass of ice and he made sure to take the jelly with him, first waving it at his neighbor and saying, "Before you change your mind."

While the man was left alone to wait with his neighbor's wife it was quiet enough for him to hear a hissing watery sound coming from behind him. When he looked toward the noise he saw a small river of water escaping out of the grass. It was gathering in a small dark puddle that was growing, gradually filling in a black hollow spot in the gray gravel driveway. The woman had turned the hose on in case there was a fire. The spray head had a bad rubber washer and leaked miserably.

When the husband returned he handed the man a fresh glass of vodka and he placed a large zucchini from their garden beneath his neighbor's chair. The man and wife had a large garden and just that spring had planted a dozen fruit trees, most of which were just out of their pink and white blossoms while others were showing their first small bearing of fruit. The couple had more zucchini than they knew what to do with.

The two men started talking but it wasn't about the motorcycle. They were seated below the spruce but they didn't talk about how the tree had gotten trimmed. The woman was trying to stand next to her husband but all her focus was on her leg which was less than a foot away from the man's arm and the fires were getting hotter, turning white within her, flashing in her eyes. She could feel in her palms the sweat of the man's mossy lower back so she stooped to give the child once again to his father. With her hands free she pushed her hair back and away from her flushed and golden face. She let her dark hair hang from her back-tilted head so she could cool without it touching her neck, and for one careless moment she looked up and tried to lose herself among the stars. When that couldn't satisfy her she tried to catch her breath before returning to her son and standing behind her husband. But from there she and the man could see the fireworks showing in one another's eyes again so she moved yet another time back behind the man seated in her chair. When that didn't work she finally put her son down onto her husband's lap and retreated into her house.

The two men could not take their eyes off the baby. They started talking about parenthood. "No one z'ever ready for their firs kid," said the infant's father. Plainly, he was drunk.

"No one can see just how much their lives and wives will change," the older boy's father agreed.

"I v'only had one kid fuh two years. But I bet I could write a book about it. There's got to a'ready be a thousan'. Maybe ten thousan' books. A'ready in print. But see the thing is...it's like that saying says... th'more things changes th'more they stay uh same. Every woman gets pregnant wants t'buy books she can read before the kid's is born. Then they read everything about the medicine."

"And they write another book."

"Egg-zackly," the host said, raising his glass as high as he could reach, making him lose his balance, nearly turning over his chair.

"What we really need is a short pamphlet that covers the basics. Like a synopsis. Like rules to a simple card game."

"Like GO FISH! Like which end is up an' when it's ok t'push in the roas beef."

Then more fireworks went off, lighting the sky like signal flares shot from a gun, and the men forgot all about raising children.

When the woman returned she tried to stand between the two men but the fireworks were still going off in the man's eyes. Shadows from the exploding arrangements of fire spilled across the ground. The quiet darkness was shattered by the light.

The woman ignored her husband when he tried to lift the baby up to her. She felt like she was still too hot to hold her child, that it could create a mortal sin if she held him now, one that she might never put down. She felt like the heat was going to break out of her in a rush to climb into the outspread arms of the tree where surely even one spark would make the whole world begin to flicker. There was a fire kindling just beneath her skin making it glow with heat and she knew all of her wetness could never quench such a fire. The sap in the tree would draw the fire under its hood where it would be quick to breach the land and break into the sky, like a rocket lifting off. The needles would be the first to go, creating a loud-crackling firestorm. Soon the small branches and then the heavier limbs would begin to sizzle, getting louder as the fire continued to ride the trails of liquefying pitch. Yellow fire would streak up the trunk of the tree and leap off the top into the purple sky. Then the outside of the house would become ablaze, and the truck that wouldn't run would appear to have all its tires spinning as the fires roared and the smell of burning rubber tainted the air. Surely the garden would wilt, the fruit trees would blacken and crisp, and all the family photos inside the house would curl into themselves until they were lost and the man's and woman's and baby's faces dissolved into ashes along with the rest of the neighborhood. Then the town would be next to burn, to turn to ash, the very last thing being the world itself. So the woman with the flushed and golden face reached down beneath the man's chair when no one not even her husband or her son or any of the kids launching fireworks could see her take back the zucchini and escape with it back into her small blue house. Once inside, she cut the zucchini in half and then she cut the halves into quarters. Then she continued chopping and mincing till nothing was worth keeping and she threw it all away.

While she was inside, the kids burned the last of their fireworks, then they disappeared into a field of moon gold grass that smelled of hay and grain silos and freedom. When the woman came back outside it was dark and quiet, except for that hissing sound. She turned off the water and the spray slowly stopped, looking as if it had been retrieved back into the hose. The woman went quickly to her husband and took up her baby and was content to hold the child while the two men continued to sit and drink, to talk till their ice was melted and the stars were covered and it was dark again.

"Welp," the husband said. I'll jus go turni-doff the hose'n...be right back."

"I already did," the woman told him.

"Di-dwat?"

"I already turned off the water. I thought you might have heard me." The woman continued to stand outside, till she could see salvation moving in her baby's eyes and it was cool enough to make everyone want to go back inside.

LIBRA

My real name is Leo. Leo Costello. My mother is downstairs eating mushrooms with some people, some friends. Psychedelic mushrooms. That's fine. I just don't agree with her decision to eat them in front of me. I'm only fifteen.

Besides, these people she's with, they've been known to get violent when they get fired up. When they get high or fried or whatever you want to call it. These friends are husband and wife. Bill and Kathy. Kathy works at the café with my mom. They're on the same shift. They cover for one another. They talk a lot. Have a good time. Sometimes too good. But, that's my view. Bill doesn't know about it. I only know by accident—details not included.

It's really Bill who's the violent one. That is, he's the one who starts it. But it's Kathy who's the one who pulled the gun in the argument over a dirty kitchen. It's Kathy who threatened to kill herself, then hid here, sleeping with my mom for two weeks. I don't jump to conclusions. They did more than sleep.

Mom's pretty open about things. Her name is Annie. We have good conversations. She's taken me to parties with her since I was ten. To be her bodyguard. I would hold her drink so she always had a place to come back to. I never took a sip until she offered it. Once I had so much I got sick, but I don't come close anymore. I'm not too good for my own good. I'm just not that interested in altering reality. I don't know that much about reality as it is.

Mom asked me to call her Annie, as if she was just a friend of mine. I did it until I was six, maybe seven. But then I decided it didn't work that way. Not for me. I needed a mother more than I needed another name to remember. So I made up my own mind. She laughed when I told her this, but I've been allowed to hold my own opinions ever since.

Leo. Mom picked my name before I was born. Way before. Obviously before she got involved with astrology—being as I'm a Libra. She'd become something she hadn't planned—a single mother. She says she's always survived best on instinct, on wit and spontaneity, on natural female charisma. When she's good, she says, she's really good. And when she's bad, she ultimately finds her best potential.

Mom keeps her mushrooms in the freezer with the rest of the frozen vegetables. She keeps her pot in the junk drawer. She pretends not to hide them, as if there's a relationship between the time it takes to find her drugs and the amount of guilt she feels for using them. Actually, this relationship exists. Mom's abusing the relationship. It's just for recreational use, she says. And it is. It's just that she's been taking a lot of time off lately. Doing a lot of recreational partying.

She's told me more than once that I could get high with her if I wanted. If I was curious. But I don't want to. I'm not saying I never will. I'm saying one day I will have to give it a try. I'm just not ready. I have enough on my mind as it is.

We're both in transition. We're both going through some changes, including Mom's separation from Richard. Richard's Mom's husband. He's been my dad for as long as I can remember. He's not exciting enough for my mom. He thought patience was a virtue. He thought quiet was good. They argued for a few weeks before they split. They didn't drag it out. But I still learned a lot of personal stuff I don't need. Stuff too personal to mention. I don't like learning things through the process of argument, even if it's not my argument.

Bill and Kathy are getting loud downstairs. I heard a chair get turned over. They've cranked the music up too loud, to where the speakers can't handle it, and the sound is all distorted. Richard didn't like loud music.

I got to meet my father once. My real father. Mom took me to see him in Seattle two years ago on my birthday. Mom said since I was thirteen, a teenager, I could have anything I wanted. That's not her regular logic. That's her way of giving me something special. Seeing my father was what I wanted. Despite her own reluctance she followed through. Mom's not one to break her promises.

That was the first time I saw her get ripped beyond control. By the end of the evening she was hanging all over both of us. My father seemed pretty familiar with that kind of behavior. He let me know the two of them had been in similar situations before. He doesn't drink, and he doesn't appreciate those who do. I think he might be an alcoholic. He stopped me from caring enough to ask. My father is not my type, but I'm glad I got to meet him. I don't think my father is the family type.

Mom was so hung over the next morning that I had to drive home—four hours on the interstate. I've never been so awake in all my life. I can still feel the incredible stretch of the passing landscape. I can still see the red eyes of the tail lights on the car ahead of me.

Leaving Richard is not an example of one of Mom's broken promises. The families we create are never as strong as the families we're born into. It's just a fact. We can't change the families we're born into. We can't go back and we can't go too far ahead of who we are or where we're from. We've got a contract with our genes. We try to renege on that contract we could get both our legs broken. I'm still part of my father's family, and I've met him only once.

Someone's turned the music back down. Must have been Mom. She's probably flaking out on Kathy and Bill. Flaking out--a reflection of Mom's astrological sign.

Being Libra, I need balance. Inside, I know what's right and wrong. I know I need to let things inside if I'm to know anything at all. My mom is Aries. She puts herself out there. Her phrase: Living Out Loud. Mom lives out loud. She is the one who turned me on to the zodiac. I think one of the reasons she's always been so open about things with me is so she can hear my opinion. She told me when I was very young that I had more common sense than she ever would.

She knows I don't agree with what she's doing downstairs. She knew this before I left the room. Mom has an incredible sense of self, but she is emotional. She leads with her heart. This often gets her involved in things before she knows what's going on. This causes her to back out on a lot of things she starts and people criticize her for being flaky. But, ultimately, it's because she has to do the right thing. So, it's okay. She'll be up here to talk before the night is over. This is what I'm waiting for.

I like my mother. That's never been a problem. But I know I don't have to like her, and I know I don't have to dislike her just to make a point.

Something Mom does not do. She does not confuse drugs for real life. She does not confuse drugs for me. She would choose me and my empty pockets every time. On this I'd bet my life.

Something new. I'm ready to move on but it's not time to go. I have two more years at home. They could be the best two years of my life or the worst. I don't know which. I'm not looking for trouble. As I said, Mom and I are both in transition. We both have to get on with the next step. We have gotten each other this far.

I think it's time for me to have a name that means something. I think it may be time for me to find my own name. Even if it's only good while it lasts. Even if it has no future. Like putting together a temporary family. At least I'll have a name I like. At least I'll have the security of the old one.

Bill and Kathy have gone. Mom has turned the music off. I hear her steps rising slowly through the creak of wooden stairs. Her bare feet slip down the dusty hall toward my door. I have no idea what mushrooms do to a person. I have no idea if we can talk or if we'll have to wait till morning. But there's one thing I must tell her, just to see how it goes, no matter what condition she is in. There's one thing that I'd like her to at least think about. I'd like her to think about a change in direction. I'm going to ask her to call me Libra from now on, at least around the house.

RECYCLING

"Get up," Angela says. "It's Easter."

I have been asleep in my recliner and though it is not yet dark I can see I have slept away the afternoon. "Since when do we celebrate Easter?" I yawn.

"Since today."

I follow Angela to the kitchen where the counter is cluttered with used glass, plastic and metal containers. Her hair is dark and her eyes are in shadow. Her mouth is a straight line stretched from end to end. She looks as if her life now lies at sunset, as if her brightest hours have passed her by.

"So, what are we doing for Easter?" I ask.

"This is it," she says, handing me a dish towel. Then everything she says I've heard before. It starts with the recycling.

I say throw it out, she says not to buy it in the first place. Like there's an unwritten rule that spouses must forever go round and round in the brittle heat of certain arguments. Our ongoing dispute is over recycling. Then something big hits the window.

I find a big black bird crumpled in a feathery pile outside the house. The mountains to the east are barely visible in the dark while the tall bay windows are ablaze with a fiery stripe that reflects the sunset. The bird has a long pointy beak and a small white patch on its chest of greasy feathers that flicker in the wind. A pink smear of blood is on the glass. I call to Angela to see if I can influence her to come outside and I poke at the bird to see if it's alive.

She flips on the floodlight and the sunset disappears. I push the bird back to its original position as Angela comes clunking around the corner wearing a pair of my work boots. The more light that shines on its feathers the more purple they appear to be. "Is it dead?" she asks. When I say that it is she steps over its body and looks down between her feet. "Is it a girl or a boy?" Before I answer Angela jumps away like a cat frightened out of its senses. One of her feet is now bare and an empty boot lays next to the bird. "It *MOVED!*" she says. Then, with one hand on my shoulder she whispers, "Touch it...."

"Let's go back inside."

"I know what I saw."

"It's the wind."

"It...moved," she says, leveling her eyes at me.

I touch it with a small stick that penetrates deeply into its feathers. Still no movement. It looks big but beneath its dark plumage it is surprisingly small. The thin toes of its feet are curled under, just like Angela's toes curl over the top of my foot.

"I've never seen a bird like this," I tell her. "Look at the feet. No webbing." It looks like a marine bird because of its oily feathers but...I don't know. "Maybe some kind of coot...some chicken of the sea." I try to laugh but Angela won't even look at me. She's looking at the bird. I want to push it around again but I can't move with Angela standing on my foot, so I reach over with the stick to retrieve the other boot. Then I poke the bird but still it doesn't move. Not a lick. Angela's eyes continue to examine the feathered pile, still looking for signs of life. "Let's go inside," I say.

"I saw her heart beat...."

"It's dead."

"I know what I saw...."

"How about I put it in a nice box and leave it in the garage overnight?"

"*A NICE...BOX!*" In my retreat I point at the small spot of blood on the glass. "Blood doesn't mean she's dead," Angela says, taking from my hand then throwing down my stick. "Blood means she's *A-LIVE!*"

"*Was,*" I say quietly. "*Was* alive."

"You don't know that."

"Look."

"Even so, I know what I saw."

"What you saw was wind ruffling feathers."

"I saw her heart beat, OK? I felt it inside me, without even touching her."

"It's gone."

"I know what I saw...what I felt."

"But you heard how hard it hit the window."

"I can't let go," she concedes, and her head bows down. "I can't give up...."

I begin to see the situation for what it truly is. I recognize Angela's broken places, how her pain rises again through scar tissue. Her deep and unforgettable sorrow washes over her. This bird has stirred up painful memories from our past. This is more about our stillborn child than a dead bird, but I must still treat it like a bird. I can't let Angela go through this pain again. Her face is so childlike, so pitiful...hopelessly hopeful, if there is such a thing. We have both tried to forget but we do not move freely from one moment to the next. We are caught in a process, a living accumulation of our past and present hurtling toward our future. Because we live with distraction does not mean we are able to forget.

My ability to watch her is being overcome by the urge to pick up the bird and run. I scoop it into my bare hands but before I can land my second get-away step Angela has me by the neck. I forgot how well she knows me.

There are times when I forget how long we've been together and that we've ever lived apart. When I look into her eyes I know getting away is impossible. She knows exactly what I'm thinking. My intention was to cut a bee-line to the garbage can as if I was heading to the garage, but instead the bird remains in my hands and Angela controls what I do with it.

She releases my neck then leans in, placing her right hand flat upon my chest. "I feel your heart," she says. "Can you?" I don't answer. The question was rhetorical yet it makes me realize I can't feel my own heart. "You listen here, mister," she continues, then she takes hold of my wrists as she looks at me, but she doesn't say anything. Instead she sees the bird that lies between us. She sees how she is holding onto me.

"Angela. It's not a little kid."

"That doesn't matter."

"It's a bird. *Just* a bird."

"IT'S A LIFE!" she snaps, startling me enough that I try to jump back but she still holds my arms. Her eyes burn deep holes into me.

"It's dead," I whisper, turning my head away, showing me that Angela is not the only one who cannot stand the truth.

"She can't be," Angela says quietly, and her lips

don't move. "Why must you take the shortest, *fast-est* route to the garbage can? It says terrible things about you. You do it with me and you don't even notice. If I thought you really cared that little about me.... If I thought you did it on purpose...." Then she releases my left arm to grab a handful of my shirt and she pushes it up just over her head but still under my chin. "I am not going to let you ignore what's going on here!"

Before admitting that I really don't know what's going on Angela releases me and stretches out her arms as if to take flight. "THERE! RIGHT THERE! HER HEART *IS* BEATING!" Yet the bird still feels boneless as a jellyfish in my hands. I did not feel the beat of its heart yet I do feel warmth coming from inside its feathers. But I can't tell Angela. If the bird's going to die it's better that she not know it was ever alive. "Come-on-come-on!" she says. "Take her inside!" She takes off running in my boots as if she's wearing snow skis toward the door then comes to a full stop. She spins on one heel to look at me, her shoulders pushed down, her hands rolled into small sharp fists. I know what's coming....

"If you do *anything* to this bird," she begins. "If you hit or kick or try to toss her in the trash, or any other awful thing…I will leave you forever. Get it?" she demands, as if she'd asked a question, as if the question was mine to answer. Again, I see how deep love can suddenly rise into a mountain of remorse.

"Got it."

"Good!" she says, happy to have so quickly reached this agreement. I realize this was the end she was looking for and the means to get here just didn't matter. I look into her eyes. I see her face. She is trembling. She wants this with her whole body, perhaps more than she's wanted anything since we lost our daughter, and it breaks my heart.

"If you want my help then do as I say," I tell her. It's easy to see that she really does trust me. "Bring me a wet towel." I have to smile so I look away.

We meet at the oven, me holding the bird, she holding a brand new cloth diaper in one hand, a tattered and burned dish towel in the other that she claims is an old wedding gift. I put the diaper down and start telling her about how I used to live next to a lake as a kid, about how my brother Mike found a baby duck and "loved the thing to death," as my mother described the incident. I tell Angela how we'd seen ducklings get run over on the road. We'd seen them get snatched by largemouth bass from below and by red-tailed hawks from above. More than once we'd seen bull frogs with little ducklings half swallowed, appearing confused about what to do with the rest. It was one of those poor ducklings that Mike pulled from the mouth of a bull frog. It looked to be dead but my Dad took and wrapped the little thing in a damp towel that he thrust into my mother's oven. Nothing happened at first, but after awhile we began to hear little chirps and taps coming from inside, and sure enough that little duckling came back to life. Like us it had been perched on the point between life and death.

Angela stands next to me in the kitchen. I handle the bird gently, wrapping it loosely in the damp towel. I pass the bundle into Angela's arms and she places it gently between the top and bottom racks to shield it from the elements. I tell her all we need to do is wait, that magic now has a chance to happen.

Her eyes are filled with hope. She watches everything I do as if my every movement, every push and pull of muscle holds something detrimental to the success of this healing magic. I'm not sure what to do so I pull the door open a little more, like she does when she broils chicken. Her eyes are so full of love and trust and high expectation that I have to leave the room.

"How come you never told me before about your Dad and that little duckling?" she asks, but there are times when the best answer to a question is no answer at all. "I like knowing that about your Dad," she says, taking a seat quietly before the oven door.

One of the reasons I didn't answer her is because Dad's not around anymore. None of his doctors had any nifty country remedies for him. Their remedies always seemed to do more harm than good. The other reason I didn't answer her is because not till after our baby was born did we know anything was wrong with her, and it's hard enough to accept the death of a child without adding false hopes before she lands. Grace *does* come under pressure, but often it leaves without notice.

*

I sneak back to my recliner in the living room. My eyes drift to the oily smudge that remains on our window. Angela's words flow over me like warm honey. I'm gazing into a cold gray TV while she still sits at full attention looking through the magical glass of the oven door, waiting for a sign. I think about telling her if the bird doesn't wake up soon to throw in a chopped onion so we don't have to concern ourselves anymore with dinner. But I don't, even though Angela knows by now when to ignore me. She knows when to laugh and when not to laugh at my foolishness. I have learned to sacrifice common sense for humor to help my Angel laugh.

I begin to imagine what the bird's reaction would be if it does wake up. Whatever cut off thought last flew through its brain between the time it hit the window and the time it hit the ground would be nothing compared to what it would think when finding itself in this cooking-cage, with some human dancing the voodoo dance blocking its only way out.

It didn't occur to me to turn on the TV. I've been content to sit here thinking about those time-less summer nights spent in the country when Angela and I were little more than kids when restlessness begins to move in around me. I start thinking about the endless argument I have with Angie over how to dispose of our recycling and I cannot help but laugh.

We never used to fight over anything, especially something so meaningless as packaging. The size of our carbon footprint never challenged the weight of our existence or the value of our relationship. Our greatest fun used to be driving around on warm summer nights in my old man's FORD, listening to the radio and the rattle of the tailgate. We would carouse harmlessly out on the moonlit roads near our home, me behind the wheel while she threw empty Oly bottles out her window at passing sheet metal signs. When she hit her mark the sound was far more impressive than that of a strange bird going all Kamikaze at a large picture window. How did we get to take so seriously those things that once made us laugh?

Angela used to smile at me and I used to smile back to her at the beginning and the end of each day as if we really knew and loved one another. Now that we think we know each other we dismiss one another like strangers. Now it's all...Did you do what you were supposed to do? And...What are we having for dinner? We go round and round over the least meaningful things for the most meaningless reasons. It's like we can't hear each other anymore. When one of us gets to talking for any length of time a dull translucent glaze washes over the other's eyes as if suddenly overcome by blindness. It only makes sense that one of us should have left by now, but we haven't.

I think it's a real shame that Angela and I may never be quite so stupid or quite so happy as we were when throwing un-recycled litter at STOP signs. When you begin to know that, well...you begin to know too much.

It suddenly occurs to me that I've fallen asleep. I hear the faint but excited voice of a long lost lover. From outside my spinning funnel cloud of sleep the voice becomes louder and more familiar. She summons me. Her call draws me in against her and I know the feel of her before we touch. Suddenly we are caught together, as if we are bound by our mutual hopes and promises, and the two of us rise as fast as if we'd fallen out a window. While we are rising up through this funnel cloud I hear Angela calling my name.

I jump up in time only to duck back down, barely avoiding getting hit by a fleeting shadow that thunders through the edge of my peripheral vision. Angela is yelling something but I cannot tell what it is. I hear feathers like wildly shaken newspaper thrashing at my ears. Wingtips skitter off the ceiling as wildly hysterical screeching rips through the room, tearing out of every corner. Somehow the sharp yellow beak misses me completely and the bird ricochets off the same damned window it hit before. But this time it rises off the carpet, taking to the air again just as Angela appears to be in slow motion.

Angela's face is flushed and smiling as her pendulously swinging hands release two oven mitts that slowly wheel through the air toward me, setting up a perfectly timed double play. They are so close and seem to move so slowly that I can see the knitted seams before they land precisely on my two outstretched hands. In the same motion, as I pluck our holy feathered Phoenix from the air, Angela opens with perfect timing the sliding glass door. When I release my grip I am at her side and we hold one another as we watch the bird, now a winding black dot being absorbed into the night sky, her cutting black wings separating us forever. Angela and I remain arm in arm. In her free hand, over our heads, she twirls the diaper, saying goodbye.

Immediately she begins to recount the tale, how it happened, when the bird awoke and started tripping drunkenly around the insides of the oven, rattling the hot metal racks. She told how she opened the oven door to have a look when the creature shot the gap and went straight for my head. She is too excited to care about me being with her from the start.

I feel a rupturing crack running through my body. It splits me open like two heavy hands ripping a watermelon in two, and out breaks the pent-up laughter that had slept noiselessly in me since just after the bird went into the oven. I hang tightly to each word of Angela's story. I am laughing at her happiness. I am laughing because while Angie was tending to the bird, before I sat down, I was tending to every piece of recycling in our place, every chunk and shred of used glass, paper, plastic and cardboard that I could find, and I sorted them neatly into her three green wicker bins.

She is so happy. I love her so much right now. I keep laughing, again and again. I can't help but imagine how she's going to yell at me for throwing away the recycling while she was sitting with the bird. She will needlessly rifle through the messy garbage where she expects to find her precious refuse, and I will let her do it. Boy is she going to be mad! But for now Angela looks into my eyes. She sees me. She touches my trembling heart.

WHO KNEW WE COULD
BE SO THIRSTY

The porch light was already on and another light was on inside. He rang the doorbell. It was nearly three in the morning. He'd called ahead so the man knew he was coming. The man opened the door right away, then he grabbed his friend by the elbow and guided him in through the door.

"Sorry to call so late," the friend apologized again. He'd already apologized on the phone.

"Think nothing of it."

"I had no place to go. I had no one to call. I have something I need to tell you."

Then the man's wife came downstairs, pedaling down in her slippers and pajamas. Her husband was in his bare feet, wearing his robe and beneath that only his underwear. She yawned but that didn't matter to anyone. She took their friend's coat and hung it over the stair rail, then she took her friend's other elbow. Like this the man and his wife walked their friend into the living room, and like that the three sat down on the couch, their guest still in the middle. Then they unlocked their arms. There was only one light on in the room, a small table lamp.

"Now tell us what this is all about," the woman said to their friend. She yawned again. She couldn't help herself.

"But I'm keeping you up. You should really go back to bed. It's late."

"Nonsense. Tomorrow's Saturday. No one here has to work," the man said.

"That's right, it's Saturday," the woman said. "It's already Saturday." She was delighted. "Tell us all about it," the woman said. "Get it off your chest."

"All we did was go out to the river to look at the birds."

"Why don't you get the man something to drink, honey. Are you hungry? You have dinner? Honey, make him some dinner. He's starving. Just look at him."

The woman stood up. "I bet you haven't eaten all day. I know I can't eat when we fight."

"When do we fight? We don't fight. Do we?"

"It wasn't really a fight," the friend said.

"I bet you haven't eaten all day," the man said. "A guy forgets to eat when these things happen."

"That's right," the woman said, acting like her husband had said it first, the thing about not eating all day. "Who could eat at a time like this. It must feel like the whole world is falling apart."

"It has."

"But most of it's behind you now," the man said. "The worst part's already over. Just a little clean up to do. Things will look much better tomorrow."

"Today," his wife corrected. "It's already Saturday, remember?"

"But first you have to eat." The man glanced at his wife. "Say, you want a drink? Bring him a drink, honey. Just look at him. Look at that face. Could that face use a drink, or what?"

"I have water or milk to go with dinner. Or I could make you some juice."

"No, not with dinner," the man said. "Right now. Bring'im the juice right now, honey." The man laughed at that one. "Bring'im a whiskey, honey. The man needs a whiskey. And hell, it's Saturday, bring me one. Thanks, honey."

"I think I'll have one myself," the woman said.

"Sure, why not? It's been awhile since we got a little pissed. Why not? It's good for us."

"Tomorrow's Saturday," the woman repeated. "So why not?"

"Tomorrow? Tomorrow's today. Tomorrow's Sunday, for crying out loud."

"Tomorrow is tomorrow," his wife said.

"You're right. Ha! You're always right. I can't seem to get it right. So what do you say to a drink?" the man asked his friend.

"Whatever you say."

"And don't forget his food," the man called to his wife on her way to the kitchen. "Bring'im some o'that spaghetti. Fill'is plate." He turned to his friend. "When we make spaghetti we make spaghetti, y'know what I mean. With plenty of leftovers. Spaghetti is always better the second day. So you'll have better than what we had earlier. Plus, food's always better when someone else does the cooking," the man said. "Isn't that right, honey?"

"What's that? What's right?"

"That food's better when someone else does the cooking? Don't ask me why. It just is."

"That's right," the woman said, now poking her head through the kitchen door. "We have all that figured out, don't we? Tell him how we figured that one out while I finish making our drinks."

"See, I make the sauce and she makes the noo-dles and the bread and the rest. We do it together yet apart so that there's always a surprise, some unknown, y'see what I mean. I do my part, she does hers, but when we sit down to eat it's like someone else did the cooking. Maybe sounds crazy, but it works. Works for us, anyway. D'you cook?"

"That's great," the friend said. Naturally he had a hard time listening. He couldn't hold his focus on anything else. The man looked at his friend, a little embarrassed, like talking about cooking was a thing too small to talk about. "No. Really," his friend assured him. "It's the small things, things like that, like cooking--those things make a difference."

"Here's to Saturday," the woman said, walking across the room with their drinks on a tray.

"Fancy," the man said. "You should come over more often, buddy. The wife's treating us like roy-alty."

"Here's a royal toast," the woman twittered. "Here's to Saturdays."

"And here's t'good luck," the man said. "To tomorrow being Saturday. See, that's good luck."

"Your luck is already changing," the woman said. "You see that, buddy."

"So tell us what happened," the man said. "C'mon, buddy."

"As I was saying, we went to the river to look at the birds. We'd been out there a hundred times. It was like any other time."

"We forgot our toast," the man said.

"That's right," the woman said. The three touched their glasses together. The friend, the hus-band and his wife all drained their glasses.

"Will you look at that," the man said. "Who knew we could be so thirsty. How about another."

"All right," the woman said. When she picked up her husband's empty glass he patted her on the behind. This startled her. He never patted her on the behind. She turned to their guest. "Should I call your wife? What's her name? I don't mind calling her. I'm sure she'd appreciate knowing you were here and you were ok."

"It's too late to call her now. But thank you."

"You don't know how women are. We worry. We'd much rather get a late night call than no call at all. If anything, we get more sleep after the call than we'd get worrying all night."

"I'll think about it," the friend said. "Thank you," he said, handing the woman his empty glass.

"Coming right up," she said. "Your dinner is warming in the oven." The woman left the room.

"We don't mind calling your wife for you."

"Julia."

"It might be too early to talk to her yourself, but we don't mind."

"It's too late to call."

"And too early to tell her you're all right. Am I right. Say, you're right--you have something there, don't you. Let'er sweat awhile. You know what I mean. It makes the comeback that much sweeter. It's good for her not to know where you are. Makes her think."

"She's not thinking about where I am."

"That's good then." The woman returned and handed the men their drinks. "Here's to a new beginning," her husband said, raising his glass.

"Wait for me," the woman said. "I left my drink in the kitchen. To a new beginning," she said upon re-entering the room. "Many happy returns and a happy ending!" They touched glasses then the woman went back into the kitchen.

"Well, let's get the worst part out of the way, shall we," the man said, turning to face his friend head on. He looked his friend in the eye. "Did either of you cheat? You know, sleep around? Did you get caught?"

"No. It's nothing like that."

"That's good. Everything can be forgiven then. It's all there for you still. It's not lost yet."

"I don't know," the friend replied. "I mean, worse things can happen."

"Nothing's worse than cheating. You can't know that because you've never done it. But it's the worst thing, the very worst thing. Cheating. Not every woman can get over that, and no man can. Not that I've seen."

"Have you cheated?"

"Of course not. Hell no. I'm still alive aren't I. Say...you haven't hit her, have you?"

"What?"

"And she's not hit you, right?" The woman was peeking in from the kitchen. She was listening but then turned away, letting the men have their say. "I hear that's a thing now. Women hitting men, and it being called spousal abuse. Never heard of such a thing myself, a woman beating a man. I wouldn't have thought it possible. So you haven't hit each other?"

"No. Never."

"That's good then."

"I guess. But I think maybe there's worse things. I mean, I pushed her, so it's me who did it."

"Nonsense. Like they say, it takes two to tango."

Then the woman came back into the room with a place mat and a plate heaped full with spaghetti. "You just stay comfortable where you are. Just eat."

"Honey," the man said. "We've been talking. What's worse than cheating on your spouse if it's not physical abuse? We can't think of anything."

"Why think of such things right now? Never mind that. I don't even want to know. Besides, he's eating."

"And I'm starting to agree with you," the man said to his wife. "I'm beginning to think we should call Julie."

"Julia," corrected the guest.

The guest tried to eat but he was obviously not hungry. He had no appetite. "That's all right, honey," the woman said to him. "Let me pick that up, get it out of your way. No one wants to smell food when they're not hungry."

"Maybe I could just go to sleep," said the guest.

"Nonsense," the man said. "The last thing you want to do is wake up tomorrow with no plan in place. Let's make a plan then get some shuteye. Otherwise there's no reason to get up in the morning."

"Perhaps he should get some sleep," the woman said as she entered the room. "Perhaps all of us should. Just sleep this off."

"I think I should go."

"Go?" the woman said.

"It's not something I can sleep off."

"Nonsense," the man said again.

"Where will you go?" the woman said.

"To find her. I left her there." He got up and walked to the door, waving goodbye but not looking at either of his friends. He waved behind his head as he walked out the door, forgetting all about his coat.

"I think we upset him. We let ourselves get into a fight," the woman said.

"We didn't fight," the man said. "When did

we fight?"

"We argued. That was rotten. What a rotten thing to let happen. To argue in front of him. We didn't even let him talk. Shame on us."

"Where will he go at this hour? I don't remember arguing."

"The only place he can go. It was nothing, nothing to worry about."

"Shame on us. Were we really fighting?"

"Not like we used to."

"What do you think happened at the river do you suppose? Did he ever say?"

"I thought he told you. When I was in the kitchen. I was going to ask--I really meant to. But I thought he told you."

There was another knock on the door, harder this time.

"Poor soul," the woman said.

"Yes. He must've changed his mind."

The man opened the door, expecting to see his friend. He didn't say anything. Then he opened the door wide enough for his wife to see.

HER HUSBAND'S FISH

The man's name was Gryphon but no one used his name anymore. Not even he thought about it except occasionally when he saw it on the mail, but then his wife's name was there too, Mr. and Mrs. He had nothing of his own. Almost everything in the mail was directed to CURRENT RESIDENT, or OCCUPANT. Nothing felt like it was his and his alone.

He found himself fishing on a small black lake at dawn. It had been years, even decades, since he had last fished this place. The lake looked the same though the black oval center of it had gotten smaller due to the weeds and lily pads now growing farther and farther out from the shore. The lake had been closing like an eye now left squinting up at the sky. He had pushed himself away from home to get there, to find some peace and quiet. During the drive he'd wished he had a boat that he could push away from shore. He had to get away from home, his wife, his life. After he'd retired everything he thought he'd been working for had turned into a trap. But as soon as he parked his truck at the familiar end of the dead end road he was set free back into a world that had been invented before his many jobs and his marriage.

How quickly he seemed to have gotten back to the end of that sun bleached log, not really a log but a weathered old spruce tree that had fallen sometime before he had ever fished this place. Its limbs were standing up out of the water, perhaps like eyelashes, with no bark on them anymore, naked and sideways to the tree but still aiming up at all angles. He stood looking at the still surface of the water, the surface like a thin black skin stretched tight as a drum between him and the fish.

The lake was trapped between the end of this gravel road and an old expired landfill. The city had dug out the dump site since he'd last fished here. Then they filled it in with dirt and tree stumps from other places and went on to build five soccer fields in its place, though even the soccer fields could not be seen from the man's position on the log. A thin scrim of red alder woods remained around the lake. A mist was hanging over the black water with shivering clouds of mosquitoes. There was no wind, nothing to disturb the still, mirrored surface. He could hear the sound of the ocean rolling over the dunes from the beach a mile away. He didn't have to abide the ripe smell of rotten garbage anymore, yet it was still with him, still in his nose somehow. Other than the ocean all he could hear was his feet quietly stirring on the log that crumbled beneath him. Occasionally there was the belly flop sound of carp clapping against the surface of the water, creating rings here and there. There was the small sound that his lures made when he cast them out upon the water and the slow winding of his reel when he pulled them back. From the trees came the kreck-eck of small frogs green and brown.

Carp.

After an hour he'd caught an assortment of pan fish--crappie and sunfish and yellow perch-- but that was not what he was after. He was after largemouth. Bass. But now that he'd seen the carp he had to think about them, too. He hadn't thought about them in years. He hadn't been fishing so he hadn't put himself in a position where he needed to think about them. The carp. They were slapping at his conscience, lunging across his mind, mouths agape. He finally said hell with it. He quit trying to hold them back. He let them in.

He and his cousin used to trap muskrat and nutria and mountain beaver when they were in high school. They thought they had gotten used to kill-ing. Sometimes they'd even laughed about it. The best bait for their trap lines in those days was carp. They'd chop the fish into soft chunks then set out the jawed traps just under the water at the end of the musky lakeside runs. The best place to locate carp was Alder Creek. This was not a small trickling crystal river running shallow over a stony bottom. It was wide, deep in places, an ancient crevice filled with brown slow moving water over black silt, though sometimes the sun could beat it into a metal gray corrugate, turning it nearly into a vision of blue, but never quite blue. They'd fish for carp often but they rarely caught them. They thought there must be better ways to hook them. Then one day his father told him to get rid of a litter of unwanted kittens.

"How do I do that?" he asked his old man.

"I don't care," the man said. "Get rid of them. Drown them if you have to."

Between he and his trapping partner they creat-ed a practical way to drown the kittens. "Why waste lives?" they said to one another. They caught plenty of carp, and they trapped plenty of nutria, muskrat and mountain beaver that year. But then they lost their taste for trapping and moved on to other enterprises to make their money. That was also the year he shot the swan and told his mother it was a snow goose so she would cook it for dinner.

But still, standing on the log, the man leaned out over the water, wondering how he could catch a bass. There was a frog in the water. The old man put down his pole and walked off the log then tried to quietly shuffle down the bank, his feet slipping noisily through the cattails and sedge and bear grass. He saw plenty of frogs, brown and green, spotted frogs and red-legged frogs and large deep green bullfrogs as well. He could hear them jumping off the bank as he approached but he couldn't see them. He saw the splash and then the ripples in the water settled and then he could see them holding tightly to the bottom. A small thing was trapped between him and the edge of the water, a small brown mouse. He didn't kill it. He picked it up by its tail. He put the mouse in his tackle box and thought about what it might look like on the water.

From the bottom of the lake, as if from behind that eye, he looked up at the surface. Small lights flickered. They pierced through the water and nearly touched the bottom. Small fish moved through the milky caramel colored light, then larger fish shimmered as they moved, sliding along. Minnows, schools of tadpoles, catfish. Larger fish cruised more slowly, down below the others. Flat-eyed bass were thrusting their tails and springing suddenly from black holes, their hiding places, taking smaller fish into their mouths, breaching out from beneath the sunken banks, out from under fallen logs and dark green clouds of lily pads flowering on the surface. The bass, large mouthed, able to take whole small ducklings paddling along the surface into their mouths. The thing about being a fish, the man thought, if you were big enough there was nothing there to hurt you. He felt the courage and the hunger. With his fisheye view, he didn't know if it looked more like earth, heaven, or hell. It remained dark with all the light above, and the small silhouette of a mouse crawling along the top.

He changed his gear, removing his lure and swivel and tied only a bare barbed hook at the end of his line. He thought about how many casts he might get out of it. Three, he imagined, that would be all the chances he would have. Then he retrieved the mouse out of his tackle box and with the hook pierced it carefully through its fur between the shoulders. Then he cast it out to the edge of the lily pads. He drew in the slack when necessary, but otherwise he allowed the mouse to swim. There was a strike, a black and green flash of tail, and a large boiling place in the water. His pole bent over, bouncing as the bass thrashed its tail and waved its monstrous head.

"How much do you think it weighs?" his wife asked.

"At least four five pounds," the man said. "Maybe more." The man looked at the fish laid out in the kitchen sink. Both its head and tail curved up opposite ends of the basin. He thought it was at least as big around as the calf of his leg, its head nearly half as big as the fish itself, its big jaw jutting out like the bucket on a tractor.

"I just can't believe it," his wife said. "I'll clean it. We'll have it for supper. After all, you did the hard part. You had to go out and catch it. I'll clean it and cook it," she said. She set an opened beer down on the table. "Here," she said, handing him a magazine. "It's your new Field & Stream, just came this morning. What a coincidence. How did you ever catch it?" she said. She stood looking down at the fish. Her back was to the man again. She was leaning over the fish laying at the bottom of the sink. "But first we need to take pictures." She picked the fish up by the lower jaw like she'd seen her husband do, her other hand holding tightly to the slippery green tail, now still, no longer thrashing.

They'd taken the pictures and he was back at the table, sitting quietly, looking at his magazine and drinking his beer. The kitchen now smelled like the lake. He knew by his wife's prolonged silence that she was dreaming up things to say. He knew he would not tell her about the mouse. He had never mentioned the kittens and he knew he never would.

The woman had finished preparing the fish for cooking. She had unzipped the belly and removed its insides. She lopped off its head. "You should be in that magazine with your fish," she said. "You're every bit as good as them and you know it. You might as well show off your fish, too. Your catch is every bit as good as theirs. Maybe I'll just send in one of those pictures myself. How about we do that? Maybe you should make up something to tell how you caught it."

The man didn't say anything.

"Oh!" she said. "What all do these things eat?"

"A lot of things," he said.

"I found a mouse. A little gray mouse inside its stomach." She took the mouse by the tail and dropped it in the trash. "Imagine. It's such a clean little mouse. What do you suppose that mouse was after in all that water?"

Again the man didn't say anything.

"How on earth did you ever catch it?" she said.

"The mouse?"

"The fish. I know how you caught the mouse. You caught the mouse when you caught the fish. How did you catch the fish?"

"You have to think like a fish."

"What does a fish have to think about?"

"You'd be surprised."

"Tell me what it's like to think like a fish."

"There aren't words," he said. "There's only pictures and no words to go with it. A fish thinks in pictures. No other way to explain it."

"Try," she said. "Tell me what it's like to think like a fish."

"No."

With his wife's back turned, while she was setting the table, he took the Polaroid pictures and buried them under the trash. They would soon eat the fish. They would throw away the skin and the head and the bones and the tail then that would be it for the fish, except for the memory. There was always the memory. His memory. When his wife finished setting the table she went back to the kitchen where hot grease spit at her when she put her husband's fish down into the frying pan.

LIPSTICK

There's really not that much to tell.

She was driving. She had to make sure she'd shed all her tears before putting on her makeup. She'd already applied moisturizer but had yet to add foundation. She was thinking how it had probably been a year since her husband had seen her in makeup, mostly because one or the other was always asleep. Their work schedules clashed that much. After applying foundation she was being especially careful trying not to stab herself in the eye with her mascara wand. There had been times after applying makeup in the car when she'd forgotten to check it. She'd wound up looking like she'd been out on an all night drunk, by the way the brush marks swerved around her eyes. She knew the car only had to jiggle the tiniest bit from the smallest bump to draw her hand offline, so she never applied eyeliner while driving anymore. She was dabbing at the ends of her lashes, flexing her whole arm as she tried not to poke the wand into her eye. She was already miffed about her hair. She had been in such a hurry to leave she forgot to tie it back. It was falling forward in her face, getting in the way. She hadn't quite acknowledged that she'd just left her husband. She hadn't even told him.

After thinking it was going to be such a big deal it wound up being nothing, or next to nothing. It all took place in less than twenty-four hours and she was hoping it wouldn't take that long to forget, the dirty end of it anyway. She drove north then she drove south. That was it. That's really all it came down to. She was only gone one night. So far she'd only seen her lover during the day. In the past month--which was the full extent of the affair--they'd only met three times and she'd never stayed overnight, not even once. She couldn't say she'd slept with him. So that's the first thing to tell. That part's probably worth mentioning. In one way it was the biggest decision she'd ever made; in another, it all could be taken away with a simple snap of her fingers. It depended on how she wanted to look at it. What came after her leaving only mattered in how it reflected on how she returned. But leaving was nothing she would ever talk about to her husband.

In order to tell her husband why she left she would have to know why herself, but she didn't, at least not till she'd decided to return. She told herself the only reason she hadn't left him before was because she had nowhere else to go. Then she found another place with another man. All she had with her were a few clothes, her bathroom things, her makeup and her pillow. She hadn't even told her new man that she was planning to stay overnight, let alone that her intention was to move in with him.

"What do you mean you aren't leaving this time?" he said.

"What do you mean what do I mean?"

"Don't you think we should talk about it first?"

"Isn't that what we're doing right now?"

"You know what I mean."

"No," she said. "I don't think I do."

At their first encounter they knew immediately that they were going to end up in bed together, and there was nothing to do about it but go. But that was it. They hadn't really talked that much. A lot had gone unsaid. She realized that now.

"Are you running from your husband or are you coming to me?"

"Can't I do both?"

This new man had never seen her without her makeup and that began to bother her. In the mean time he was trying to figure out a way to tell her that a past girlfriend was scheduled to stay with him the following night. He was trying to tell her that when she stayed with him, though they still slept together, they were no longer physically or romantically involved.

"It's not that kind of relationship. It's no one you need to worry about," he said.

"Then why were you keeping her from me?"

"Why would you want to know about her? I knew the thought of her would only get under your skin. Plus, to tell you the truth, I really didn't think you'd believe me."

"Shouldn't I have the opportunity to make those decisions on my own?"

"Fine. Be here tomorrow night. You can sleep in the middle."

"Do you really expect me to believe all this?" she asked.

"I neither expect you to believe nor do I expect you not to believe. That's entirely up to you. All I can do is tell you the truth."

"I want to trust you. I want to believe you."

"Then do what you want. You would be right to do what you want." She was rapidly blinking her eyes, trying not to ruin her makeup. "I don't know why you let this upset you so much, but I'll tell you why I think it upsets you. Because you've had past relationships with guys who have been unkind and untrue. Because they were trying to hide something, but I'm not hiding anything."

"You were."

"I wasn't hiding it, I just wasn't talking about it. Now I'm talking about it because you want to know. It's ok for you to know, if that's what you want. If you can handle it."

"Does she try to have sex with you when you sleep together?"

"No. We sleep. Although, for a long time, before you came along, it was me who was trying to have sex with her."

"I don't like having to imagine another woman in our bed."

"It's not like that. Stop thinking it's like that. Your imagination is working against you. Against us."

"Us?"

"You and me."

"You don't know me at all, do you?"

"That's what I've been trying to tell you."

Despite the negative reflection it cast on herself she decided she could never be involved with anyone who would sleep with another man's wife.

That night she slept with him purely because she wanted to. They stayed up half the night talking, solely because she wanted someone to talk to, and that's when she realized it wasn't something her husband did that made her leave, it was something he didn't do--at least not anymore. It became as clear to her as a blue and open sky. She missed what they didn't do most of all. In some ways, this thing remembered, this talking in bed, it was all she thought her marriage would ever need, because it would open a door to everything else. Of course her new guy wanted to do everything in bed, while talking and while not talking. It was through their talk that she realized what it was about her husband that she missed, something that she missed so much she was willing to go back to him to see if they could find themselves again. It had become all too clear to her that she didn't want to be with this other guy anymore. In the morning he went to work while she stayed in bed till late in the afternoon. She showered and scrubbed her face. She gathered up her clothes and her pillow and the rest of her things. His sheets were left streaked, dotted and smeared with make-up, but her body simply dissolved and disappeared.

She knew the lights would be off and the curtains would be drawn and her husband would be in bed, but she wasn't going to let him go back to sleep, not after waking him. She wouldn't allow him to sleep till after they talked about the thing they'd never talked about before, till they talked about why they didn't talk to one another anymore. She wanted to talk about how they could remain who they wanted to be without slowly slipping into something they didn't, something terrible and dull and selfish. Then if they had to they could talk about what it would be like to never talk to one another ever again, because that's the way they'd been headed the day she left.

At first she'd decided not to put on any makeup but then she applied a little lipstick because she thought the taste of it alone might carry them back together. She knew he would most likely be holding a grudge due to her disappearance, but there remained a chance he would not even know that she'd been gone. If he noticed and if he persisted in wanting an explanation she had already prepared her answer. "No reason to involve my friends," she would say, and that would be all there was to that. Of course she knew better than to tell him the truth, about having been with someone else, because if she told him the truth they would never get a second chance. And she knew their second chance was going to be far better than their first.

She knew her lack of makeup would not matter in the dark. What she didn't know was how he would see her once the lights came on. But he, if anyone, deserved to see her as she was. She was still driving. She hardly recognized herself in the rearview mirror. She had to wonder if her husband would recognize her when the lights were on. She felt like she'd been away such a long, long time. She'd changed so much while she was gone. She had so much she wanted to talk about. The only thing left to explain would be the makeup and lipstick still running across her pillow.

ZELLERI

You think she looks like Katharine Ross in that old train-robbery-western with Paul Newman and Robert Redford playing Butch Cassidy and the Sundance Kid. She is so beautiful it hurts to look at her. The pain takes you to a place you did not know you had. You said she was that kind of beautiful, with the cool night running long through her hair and the Mexican sun rising in her cheeks. Online she called herself Zelleri and you liked it so much you didn't care if it was a name given to her or if she took it for herself. When you looked it up you found it meant one seeking love always and continuously. Then you read in her profile that she was looking for a partner but remained dedicated to the two she already had, and that made you stop in pieces, banging to a halt like a train. Then you poured on the coal to keep on going because you knew she could take you places you'd never been.

It was her idea to meet on a train. So tonight when she comes you've agreed though it's at your house you'll both pretend to be riding a downbound train, passing through beautiful old-west towns and dark countryside. She knocks once and you think you can hear the hush of the door sliding open, the sound of the wind ducking with her into the kerosene light. She is walking down the aisle, her arms up for balance, tipping from side to side as she dances toward you.

"I can't remember the last time I was on a train," you say, and when the two of you embrace it's like you've caught something so essential in your arms you can't let go.

"You'll never forget this time," she says, and when she winks it looks so natural it's like she's winked at you before. "Let's not think about where we're going. Let's not mention where we've been," she says. "We can be whomever we choose. We can go wherever we want." You think back to the first time you lay with her, how you wondered if you'd ever get a second chance to make it right, and you will.

You have ordered for dinner her favorite meal, whole Dungeness crab with tossed salad and garlic bread. She says she likes to eat with her hands. She says she'll drink just about anything. She says you're the one with whom she's willing to try everything. Immediately you take your seats in the dining car, sitting across from one another at a table that has been waiting just for you. Three tall white candles light themselves. There are waiters now, three of them dedicated to serve you your meal. You ask for wine and it magically appears.

Occasionally she mentions something that passes by the window but every time you look it's already gone. She says, "I want you to see snow. I want you to see a deep valley with an all-white sky and snow-covered trees that roll on forever. An ocean of snow," she says.

"I'm ready when you are," you say.

She begins counting. "One...two...three." You look out the window but all you see is darkness. Up closer you see the reflection of yourselves, glowing there in candlelight, still looking like there's no place else you'd rather be. This is exactly how you thought the night was going to go and it does. But then in your own reflection you see that you're still waiting for her to arrive.

The first thing she told you was that her real name was Tamara and you recount your disappointment. Tamara means Palm Tree and you just couldn't make something meaningful out of it, not like you did when her name was Zelleri. Now when you imagine her she's always wearing coconuts and her hair reminds you of Tina Turner's. You can't see that the true definition of her is standing in this woman before you. You refuse to give up on the woman you'd imagined, and you do not realize this alone could be the reason for your imminent demise. You hear yourself with all three waiters coughing one-two-three-four in the background, trying to give back what she has told you, that she got the name Zelleri from a type of fungus. You used to think for lovers and husbands and wives to be true to one another they had to love all of one another but Zelleri has shown you that you don't.

You remember the first time you lay in bed with her. It was dark and quiet and both of you were wide awake, each wondering how long it would take before you'd get a second chance. You came home once to find her cooking dinner in your kitchen. It was a complete and utter surprise. You did not know she'd be in town. "If you're too busy right now," she told you, "we can eat, have sex, then I'll go on home."

"What's cooking?" you asked.

"Chicken," she said. "Wanna neck?"

That was the first time you felt your pulse tapping so fast the beats nearly touched, typing out a line that told you that you really loved her, and why not? Your dishware, your pans and your silverware are all a function of your past relationships, gathered in an odd collection that allows everyone to pick out their favorite dish, bowl, fork, spoon and glass. Whether it is a 16 ounce Mason jar or a butter plate turned out by your son in his pottery class everyone gets something they truly want. She's been telling you for some time now that every day is a perfect day for something.

She says she likes that you can go all day without caring to comb your hair and you tell her that you love how she puts herself together. With casual aplomb she tells you she needs you to show her on paper that your doctor has deemed you free of STDs, and she says for that she will show you hers. You tell yourself that you are overexcited, but you have seen in her eyes that there is no such thing. You realize before meeting that a third of her is better than all of you but you are saved by the freedom to only show your best. And isn't it ironic that you feel three times as secure with her than you've ever felt with a woman before? You asked yourself if you could be fully satisfied with a part time relationship yet you'd already taught yourself that full time ones were not for you. You knew she would know you well enough to tell you all you yearned to hear, and she has. You know your best one-third is better than the two-thirds your former wife had pulled halfway out of you before leaving you for dead.

Now you feel bright and alive; Zelleri is three times the woman you thought you'd ever have. You've known jealousy before, but now strangely you feel none. Jealousy is a rot, a dying, a ruin. But so far you've felt no jealousy and you waste no time trying to figure out why. When she leaves at the end of the day, no matter how long she is gone, when she returns it is as though she only left that morning. In fact, in some ways, knowing she has other lovers lessens the pressure on you because you know you do not have to satisfy all of her; and after all, isn't that the point? You were so relieved the first time you heard her say I LOVE YOU because you knew she would never have to know the parts of you that she didn't.

What you never liked about online dating was having to look at so many women who only saw the differences that would keep you apart. But Zelleri makes you feel complete, a perfect match in an imperfect world. It was not all or nothing with her. It was putting your best foot forward then dis-appearing before the moon was full.

When you were in bed with her for the first time you worried you would be thinking more about her other lovers than you would about her, even though you knew she was all you wanted to see. So what you did was to describe her body in full detail, out loud so she could hear, just trying to hold your attention in check. The more you told her the more both of you relaxed. She liked to see how you saw her. There were some things you only whispered in your mind. You said, "You're mine. I can't believe you're mine." And she was, for that moment, yours all yours and everything you ever wanted.

Somewhere inside you know she'll be with you in the morning. Then you wake, as if startled from a dream. You begin to think this whole relationship is one of compromise but your heart has never felt so full. You see her dark silhouette lying against the sky like mountains arranged at a distance. Behind her is a large window, bright with the new morning's light. One naked breast rises from her silhouette and drives up into the sky. Birds fly curiously around the burnished peak of her areola as blues and greens flood back through the window. There's nothing more you need to see to know how much she's there.

You imagine introducing her to your mother, how you would feel free of all trepidation as to what it could possibly mean. Because you know what it means, even if your mother lacks the compunction to not talk about the chances of you two being married.

"I might be too much woman for him," she tells your mother, but right then she only has eyes for you.

"More like too much man," you say, and you do not regret having said it because regret no longer exists.

You can't imagine yourself being happier. You tell her you feel like you are holding hands with the tip of an iceberg and you know she knows exactly what you mean. You try not to ask yourself how long it's going to last because you already know no one will love you more than this. You are not like ships or trains passing in the night. You are on the same track, in the same train, moving warm beneath your lover's skin.

You know the table in the dining car remains set for two even though you've long since closed your eyes. Then you look out the window looking for snow but all you see is you. You tell yourself that what you don't have should be easy to forget. She was just like you imagined, but you imagined she'd be real. Yet you still think what you have today is far more real than what you hoped for yesterday. You see yourself slumped down in your chair, your head nearly touching the table. You think you hear the whistle again of that downbound train, a train that might still be yours. You want to look out the window, hoping to see its oncoming light. There's no way you are going to let her see you like this because this has no part in your better third. So you sit up. You begin rocking from side to side. You want to look for her outside in the snow. You want to listen for the sliding door and you want to smell the smoke from the kerosene lamps, but you cannot look because you know if you don't she will always be there.

WHEN I SAW YOU RUNNING

The man settled on an uphill grade, stopping his truck below his boy's mother's new place. He did not sound his horn. He sat and waited for his son to come out. He had no choice but to look over her new life. And there the bastard was, where he always was when the man came for his son, the other guy--the man's replacement--seated on the porch somewhere back in the shadows, watching the man looking for him, sporting that black porno mustache. He had sometimes worried about his wife hooking up with a better man, better than he had been, because in comparison his own flaws would seem that much larger in her eyes. But this one on the porch was not the better man, this one wagging back and forth in his sleazy porno mustache.

It was just after dawn but it was easy to feel that a hot afternoon was already on its way. The man watched a small whirling dervish crossing the road, picking up leaves like houses in a cyclone, then throwing them down. It was the Labor Day weekend and the normalcy of rain would return soon to the north Oregon coast. The boy's mom was first, then the boy, pedaling down the front steps after her, like the cavalry.

"He loves you," the woman said. "You know that don't you? He still looks up to you...."

"Well...he's shorter than you."

"Oh Frank," she said. "Can't you hear how mean you are? At least you used to try to hide it, but now.... Do you still think this is something new?"

"Don't. Not in front of him," the man said, referring to their son. "And him either," he continued, throwing his chin toward the porch. She took in a deep breath slowly then let it break out suddenly, as was her habit when talking to the boy's father.

"Last thing, Frank. Whatever you do, he thinks it's ok for him to do too, Frank." He looked at his son settling into place, buckling his seat belt. "You know there's things you do that are not ok. You know that, right?" She gave the man a pained, almost embarrassed look that the boy could not see. From the corner of the man's eye he could see the black porno mustache winding back and forth across the porch, moving in and out of the shadows. Several times, too many now to count, he had told her it was only adding insult to injury to expose the kids to her boyfriends. The guy with the porno mustache she claimed was only her second but Frank could not stop himself from imagining many more.

She said she wanted to save the boy and his sister from the details of their parents' failed relationship, but Frank thought what she was really doing was dropping his kids in a blind alley where they would be doomed to make the same mistakes. Frank did not wait for her to step away from his truck. He released the clutch to let it roll backwards before he proceeded to head up and over the hill. As he'd allowed the truck to roll down with gravity he'd felt the presence of a surreal shift and allowed the truck to drift back as if he were in a slow moving stream, like a tree that had swayed to give up its purchase from the soil, and when it let go of the earth the woman remained rooted beside the road, waving goodbye.

Often when his mind became entangled with thoughts of his marriage he looked to memories of Maggie to unfetter his mind. They had been in junior high and high school together, wrapped together into something bright that had also failed. But they did not fail the way his marriage had failed. What had occurred with Maggie remained bright somehow, gift wrapped by nostalgia perhaps, but still.... It was what it was. Sometimes he longed to tell her that she'd been right, that he was unable to forget her. Then he remembered that she was married to that ambulance driver. The stress from his current circumstances left him thinking of Maggie more and more, even though he accepted that his thoughts had nowhere to go. At least they were still around when he needed them.

The sun was already burning up the east, brightening the western skies. He had awakened to the waning purple glow of bay windows in the old family house. He witnessed the cloud-powdered azure of the open sky. But then he remembered where he was and that he was alone and his hope drained down through the same black filter that had swallowed so much of him already. He knew having his son along would help him to forget.

Beach conditions could not have been better for clam digging. The outgoing tide was still widening the beach and the waves were low and calm. The skies were blue and without wind and a round yellow sun was rising. This was the day Frank had chosen to walk barefoot with his son, teaching him how to dig razor clams in the surf. A new stainless steel shovel rocked in the truck's bed as the tires left the last of the asphalt, the truck shaking its way down a short stretch of concrete washboard. The access dropped from there, passing through the low dune ridge. Frank looked out at the sandy plain laid out before them. They were only fifteen minutes from the house. "Your mom says you worry about me cause I'm alone. She says you stress and that's why you've been biting your fingernails. What do you have to say about that?"

"I say I can handle a lot more than she thinks."

"I said the same thing. So quit biting your nails. You're making us both look bad." The man's phone was barking, a ring tone he'd set for his ex. He put his phone to his ear. "I know," he said.

"Are you talking to me?"

"Yes."

"Anyway.... Don't be late, he has school tomorrow. He needs to be home in time for dinner."

"I know," the man said again.

"I've been getting letters from the bank too, Frank. Copies of what they send you about your boat. Back payments. I know you're losing it and I'm sorry."

"Haven't lost it yet. It doesn't concern you, except you're the one taking the money I used to pay for it."

"Frank," she said.

"Stop saying my name so much. It's annoying. I know who I am and if you can't remember, that's your problem. By the way, you're on speaker," he lied. "Don't you want to say hello to your son?"

"I love you Boy-O," she said into his ear. "Have a great time with your dad. Gotta go...." The man put his hand on the wheel to turn toward the thin spread of salt water.

"You and Mom fight more now than when we lived together. What does divorce fix anyway?"

"Don't know yet. It was supposed to mean there was nothing left to fight about." The man took the truck out of gear and turned the engine off. They were slowly coasting down the gentle downward slope toward the ocean.

"And Dad, Mom gave me a card to give to you. You want it?"

"Is it a bill?"

"No. She said she's trying to be nice."

Frank didn't want to read the card. All curiosity about anything regarding her only led to anger. To him anything nice she had to say was just a small hole that she would eventually tear into a bigger one. He dropped the envelope over the back of the seat. Then he saw a redhead in red boots kicking up water as she was walking in from one of the sand bars.

"See that gal there in the red boots?" The man pointed. "The one there with the long hair?" The boy nodded his head. "That's your real mother."

"And you're making this up because…?"

"Because one night she got me drunk, had her way with me, and before I knew it I was pregnant with you. It's just time to tell you the truth."

"Yeah, well it doesn't work that way."

"Care to enlighten me on how it does work?"

"No. But I know."

"Just checking. Just making sure you have all your birds and bees in a row."

"I guess. Who's the lady in the red boots?"

"Don't know, but I'd sure like to try her on for size. If I did know her I would call her Hope, because every time I looked at her she would fill my eyes with hope. Plus it looks like she has some nice warm puppies."

"Puppies?"

"She looks like one hell of a swimmer, doesn't she? Look at that set of lungs on her. Why don't you go play in the ocean while I take her home for a swim?"

"And Dad? You say her name's Hope?"

"Yes."

"Well good, because Hope's walking straight at us." Sure enough, the red head in the red boots was sauntering right up to the truck, her waist net laden with clams. "I thought you said you didn't know her," the boy said, and he pressed himself back into his seat.

She walked casually up to the passenger side of the black pickup as if she'd done it a hundred times before, but she did not lean inside and she did not see the boy. She locked her shovel between her crossed legs and draped her hands like small brown towels over the edge of the window frame, leaning back toward the water. There was a light breeze backing her and the air inside the truck began to fill with her sweet, refreshing scent.

"So how's it hangin' over here, Frank?"

"Ok. You?"

"You know, happy as a clam at high tide."

"The red, it looks great on you."

"It's a change."

"Hi," the boy said, now suddenly in the window frame. "Nice clams." She was not one to show when she was startled.

"Where on God's green earth did you come from?"

"Ask my Dad. We were just talking about that."

"Where'd you find this kid, Frank? He's kind of tough lookin'. Are those scars or dimples, kid?" The boy stuck out his right hand.

"My name's Chance."

"Hello, Chance," the woman said, officially shaking the boy's hand. "Nice to make your acquaintance. My name's Maggie."

"MAGGIE? Are you sure?"

"That's what most people call me."

"My dad was just talking about you and he said your name's Hope. He SAID he didn't know you, sooo…I don't know."

"Your dad's getting old, that's all. See all that gray hair he's trying to hide under his hat? He's kind of a mess but don't hold it against him. He means well. Besides," she looked sideways at Frank, "you sure he was talking about me?"

"Un-questionably. Red boots, red hair, pretty…some other stuff."

"Ah shucks, Frank. You think I'm pretty?"

"He says you're a good swimmer."

"Does he, now? Well, perhaps his memory is not as bad as I thought."

"I still don't know why you called yourself Maggie or whatever."

"What I don't know is why he called me Hope. Or whatever." Chance shook his head as if he had sand in his hair.

"You guys are hard to understand."

"Looks like you didn't have a hard time getting your limit," the man said.

"You mean these little puppies?" she said standing up, stretching, arching her back and looking down at her catch. All Chance could see through the window were her breasts. "These are what your dad's been talking about when he says he didn't get any. Wanna touch'em?" The boy looked at his dad with his eyes stretched wide open.

"Don't worry son," the man said, "one day you'll get some and they'll be even bigger than hers." The boy couldn't stand it any longer and began to clumsily cover his face with the backs of his hands.

"Did I miss something?" Maggie asked, leaning into the truck.

"Nope," the boy said, now laughing even harder. "You aren't missing an-y-thing!"

"Hmmmm…" Maggie said. Then she saw the shovels in the bed of the truck. "Well, well…. Looks like *someone's* got a spanking new stainless back there. You wait any longer it's going to be too late to use it, Sleepy Head."

"That's my dad's."

"Both of'em?" Chance sat up and stretched his neck trying to see over the back seat.

"Yesterday was his birthday," the man said. "That's his gift but he hasn't seen it yet."

"Oops," Maggie said.

"You told me we were going to share *your* shovel," Chance said, then he rolled over the back of the seat and squeezed through the sliding window. Maggie was still standing at the passenger door. She patted the window frame with both hands as she prepared to go.

"Well…I've done enough damage for one day. Glad you got t'see me, Frank. Have fun swimming. Try not to drown yourself."

Red boots at night sailor's delight, he thought. Red boots at morning…. Frank told himself again that there was nothing between him and Maggie, not anymore. Whatever they'd had they left in Bankowski's barn, and that was that. He could think about her however he wanted when she wasn't around but he needed to not carry that fantasy into the few occasions when he got to see her. Maggie was married to that MEDIX driver and nothing was going to change. The part that he could have of her was only memory and fantasy and he knew it. She was the woman on his mind when he needed someone close to him. And that was all.

The man looked at his rear view mirror to keep an eye on his son. He kept seeing the oddity of the back of the boy's swaying head as they rolled down the beach. For some reason this made him laugh. He kept smiling as it occurred to him just how easy it was to love him.

The man checked his mileage and slowed to a stop. A red pickup was parked at the edge of the water, near to his usual digging spot. The boy poked his head through the window, now pointing his finger toward the red truck. "There's someone in the water," he said.

"Where?"

"Between that truck and the great big sand bar."

The man took his binoculars from beneath the seat. "There's two," he said. He threw his binoculars down and told the boy to hang on. The truck's engine roared and the body shook as the tires fought for traction. The boy could not help himself from sliding back against the closed tail gate. The truck lurched across the sand then fell to a hard stop that hurtled the boy up against the cab this time. A string of deep tide pools barred further passage.

"What's wrong?" the boy asked. In one motion the man turned off the engine, turned on his emergency flashers, opened his door and tossed his cell phone at the boy. "Someone's drowning. Call 911. I don't want you down there! You understand!" He didn't wait for his son's reply.

The man was running harder than he'd run in 20 years, so long ago that he was unfamiliar with the bouncing of his gut when he ran, and it bothered him. He crashed into a tide pool that was waist deep and pulled him down. He saw that one of the people in the water could not help himself enough to even hold up his head. The man who had been swimming tried to stand up when he got into the shallows but he was exhausted. He had a red beard and a black stocking cap while the other man was nearly bald, much older, heavier and unconscious.

"He's not breathing," the bearded man said as he continued to gasp for air. "I think he's dead." He was holding the old man's head in his lap to keep it out of the water. His arms were too weak to hold him up anymore. He was too tired to move. Frank grabbed the old man beneath the arms and tried hard to pull him onto the hard sand but he was too heavy for Frank to move by himself. Then someone grabbed onto the old man's slick rubber waders with him. Both were looking for better handles but they pulled with what they had. Together they pulled the old man up the beach till both feet were clear from the chilling water. All the man saw of his helper was her feet because he had to keep his head down while pulling, but he recognized the red boots.

"Now you glad t'see me?" Maggie said.

"Every time," he admitted. "The guy who brought him in. That guy in the beard there. He thinks he's dead."

"We're not qualified to make that decision. We have to start CPR and hope he snaps out of it. Has anyone called MEDIX?"

"Chance did. While I was running down here."

"He's a good boy. When I saw you running-

-that's when I knew something was wrong. You ready? You want top or bottom? Blow or pump? It's all the same. We'll need t'switch soon anyway…. Hey!" Maggie called to the bearded man. "We're going to need backup so don't go away." Cars were now stopping, they were collecting in a half moon around the man, the old man and Maggie. People were getting out of their cars, inching their way in, making tighter standing half circles. A group was running up the beach, along the edge of the water, toward them, throwing down everything as they ran.

"Uh-oh," Maggie whispered. "Looks like family."

"That's what I always say," the man said.

"Just don't say anything about his condition. You got me? Especially about being dead. That's the last thing family needs to hear—this is tough enough as it is." More people took to their knees, at a distance.

"Did you say dead?"

Maggie was tilting the man's head back. She cleared his tongue from his throat. "Well. It's best for everyone to think he's still alive, including me." Sea green effluvium foamed down the old man's cheek from both his nose and mouth. "Let's go to work," she said. "You trained?" She pressed warm air into the old man's lungs. He was clean shaven which gave Maggie some relief.

"A long time ago," the man said, pushing down on the old man's heart.

"Wonderful. We make a great couple." Maggie breathed in. She breathed out.

"That's what I was telling my son."

"Easy boy, can't you see my hands are full with this one?"

Their conversation was a staccato exchange passed between one another while offering breath and life to the old man.

"Shouldn't we roll him to his side? See if some water spills out?"

"Great idea," Maggie said. Maybe I *should* keep you around.... I'm playing."

"I know. I like you. You come here often?"

"No. In fact, next time...I'll pick the place," she said, now looking at him. "Hey. Better not look at him. Better keep looking at me cause this guy's changing color."

"Easy. You've always been easy t'look at."

"Ah," she whispered. "Told ya you wouldn't forget. Let's see if we can roll this guy over. You ready?"

"Ready." Each got a firm grip, one pushing and the other pulling. But the heavy body would not budge. The weight of him had settled into the wet sand.

"You, you, and you," Maggie commanded, pulling three men from the crowd. "Help us roll this guy onto his side. HURRY!"

"His name is Frank," offered one of the women. Her voice was low, mild. Maggie immediately looked to Frank, her Frank. She wanted to say something about how lucky he was not to be the Frank lying on the ground, but it was a bad time for her to make that comparison. The woman who identified the older Frank had been standing closer to the action than the other watchers. It was all she had to say.

After the three assistants had gotten Frank to his side they stepped back, anxious to rejoin the crowd, rubbing sand from their hands. Not a lot of fluid came out so Maggie and Frank moved quickly to regain their CPR positions. Maggie did a quick sweep with her elbow across the old man's mouth and nostrils to do away with the foam. Then she closed her eyes. She imagined pushing life into the old man's lungs. People whispered, talking among themselves. Others cried or even wailed. The man continued to push at the cold that tried to settle into old Frank's heart. The ocean was quiet to some, invisible to others, and still to others, roaring. The man continued to drive his weight down onto his folded hands. People could not help imagining that they were him. He continued to use his weight to rhythmically press down on the drowned man's heart, each press creating an ever increasing pain in his own left arm.

One of the wailing bystanders had been the old man's son, who had become overwhelmed by the suddenness of his father's drowning--made more shocking by the fact that the entire family had been present on this, their annual Labor Day weekend trip to the coast. He broke from his wife and children then rushed to get to his father's side. He wound up kneeled down in the water below his father's booted feet.

"Come on, Dad," he said. "You can do it. Please, Dad!" He put his head down upon his shaking hands and prayed. His voice gradually became louder, as he gave away more and more control. "God. Please, God!" he pleaded. "Oh...God! Come on, Dad!" People turned away, and the tide turned, too. The rising water was crawling under and around the old man, as Frank and Maggie labored still to save him. The son seemed to take no notice of the water's wet chill as it washed through his clothes.

The onlookers, three deep now, built of tourists and locals alike, were wedged in like bricks, creating a tight wall. Then around this wall was a larger ring of scattered shovels, along with milk jugs, plastic buckets and nets all holding clams, as if they were gathered up there as part of some saving sacrifice offered in exchange for the old man's life. Seagulls picked at the clams that lay exposed on the ground and were becoming increasingly brazen as they poked nearer and nearer toward the back of the crowd.

Maggie was beginning to have trouble with the pace. She was becoming irritable due to the ever present sand, the way it built into a grit between her teeth, the way it mixed with foam. She'd known all along that the sand was going to cause problems. It always did. There was no getting around it.

This grit was also in the old man's eyes. The pale of his rigor-worn face was undeniably grisly to all who saw. On top of that was the plain truth that the vigorous attempt to save his life had so far yielded no reward. Each thrust down upon his heart, each forceful injection of breath, each hope to overcome negative circumstance seemed to fall short of its mark. Maggie continued to look for a clean surface or piece of material upon which she could remove the miserable sand from her mouth and hands. Eventually she reached inside the victim's outer shirt to find relief by using his wet but otherwise clean undershirt, which was miserably cold. Then she went back to work.

"She must have felt a heartbeat," said a voice in the crowd. "He must still be alive." But another said, "No," which angered Maggie on behalf of Frank's family.

"Shush!" she barked. "Does anyone have fresh water? Please."

The bearded man's fingers, ears and face were purple from his exposure to the chilled water. The old man's lips were darkening, turning black. High up, white summer clouds moved, their reflection sweeping across the old man's eyes.

Maggie was behaving like a champ, but she was coming to realize more and more how physically impossible it was becoming for her to continue. She could barely push air into the old man's lungs and what she did have to offer was becoming increasingly short. She looked across at her partner whose tempo was also slowing. Both were in need of relief. Frank knew when Maggie looked at him she was asking to switch places. He knew it couldn't be him who could relieve her. "I can't," he said. "I'm sorry. I have only one lung," he lied. "I couldn't help him if I tried."

"Getting dizzy," Maggie said. "Feel like I'm going to pass out." In her red boots and red hair and all the memories he had of her, he wanted to somehow defend her. She looked abused.

"YOU!" Frank directed, coming down on the man with the red beard. "Get over here." When Maggie rose to allow Red Beard to take her place the crowd burst into applause. A young girl still winded from running arrived with a gallon jug of fresh warm water.

"You're a life saver," Maggie said.

"I hope so," said the girl.

Frank's arm was killing him, and he laughed at the irony. There was a pain growing inside his armpit. He thought he might die while trying to save a dead man. And that would be a major rip off, no matter how one looked at it. Red Beard had stalled before he got started. He seemed unwilling to perform the job. He was closing his eyes to old

Frank's face but the vision had already gotten inside his head. There was growing at this close range an undeniable look of gore. Then a heaving rush of saltwater. Frank's son sat like a stone at his father's feet, gripping his father's right rubber boot, oblivious to the waves that shot up his back. All but his lips remained still, as he continued talking to God. His father's left boot rolled back and forth with the ebb and flow of water, like a log persuaded to turn in the current.

While Maggie took a few moments to wash the sand and grime from her and Frank's faces Red Beard had time to speak and make his suspicions known. "Are you people sure you called the right number for the ambulance?" Several people replied to the affirmative, excluding Chance who was no longer in the truck but milling carefully through the crowd out of his father's sight.

Red Beard stood up. He wanted to take control as a means to escape. "Come on, we've got to pull him up from the water again." So they dragged the man up and away from the cold ocean.

Frank continued to knead at the old man's heart. "We can't stop till the medics get here," Maggie said.

"She's right," Frank said.

"FUCK!" yelled Red Beard, who had not contributed a single breath. "GOD! Where's the damned medic!"

"I will volunteer. I will take over the mouth-to-mouth if this man will not take his job more seriously," the quiet voice of a much older man came from somewhere in the crowd.

"I'm the one who pulled him from the damn water," Red Beard said in an attempt to absolve himself. But by the faces in the crowd he saw that his trial was not finished. "I'm on it!" he replied. "I'm doing it...." He pinched closed the nose, then his own eyes, and he tried to seal his mouth over the old man's. But his chest did not rise. Yellow sputum sprayed out from between their mouths. With his right hand Red Beard tried to lift old Frank's neck to tilt the head back in order to clear the airway. But the man's head and neck and body, overweight and wracked with cold, seemed to be all of one piece.

"I have an idea," Frank said, looking to Maggie to support him. She took over, pumping down on the old man's chest, putting all of her weight into it. She caught a glimpse of Chance standing in the crowd. She did not know he was not supposed to be there. He put his right index finger over his lips.

When Maggie took his place Frank slid over the sand on his knees to position himself at the head of the body where he began to dig sand out from under its head, creating a hole that would allow it to tip farther back, hoping thereby to clear the air passage. The family approved.

Sand was packing in under the man's nails. He continued digging with both hands as fast as he could, but the deeper he got the greater was the water that rose into the vacancy. "That'll have to do," he said, and for the moment he sat back to observe the scene around him. He did not see his boy. "I need your coat," Frank said to Frank's son, the man at the old man's feet. Frank took the coat and laid it over the hole before setting in the head, in order to keep the water out of the old man's ears.

The woman who had first spoken old Frank's name had resettled into a nearby place, down on her knees. She had appeared to be talking quietly to herself, as one praying. After listening more care-fully the man noticed she had not been praying but talking to the older Frank. She wore yellow rubber boots over pink sweatpants. From her waist hung a white plastic bucket. In her hands she held two small sand dollars, as smooth and green as old copper coins.

"I can't imagine what's taking him so long," Maggie said, looking up and down the beach for her husband.

Frank continued to look at the woman with the sand dollars, until she noticed him doing so, then he beckoned her to come closer. He invited her to take a place near the end of Frank's outstretched right arm, his palm still opened up to the sky, fingers curled, his hand quite empty. The man saw that inside the woman's bucket she had many more sand dollars. He reached out and held the woman's hand. She was not wearing a wedding ring. He took the woman's hand and put it together with Frank's.

No one noticed when the woman transferred the small green sand dollars into the drowned man's hand. Down below the old man's feet his son looked to the north. Immediately everyone followed his gaze, but there was nothing there. No ambulance was coming. It was just sand and water, held at a greater distance.

Maggie and Red Beard were still working, but at a slowing pace, one that gradually allowed the crowd to recognize the truth of the outcome. "We need to make a decision," said Red Beard. "We can't do this all day. I can't. We need to take a vote." So the three of them, Red Beard and Frank and Maggie, leaned in where others could not hear. Quickly they came to a 2-1 decision to keep working, with Frank replacing Maggie and Maggie replacing Red Beard. Then someone noticed a county sheriff's car skimming toward them across the beach from the north.

Then someone else noticed a red rotating light coming up on them from the south. Half cheered while the other half knew better. Frank and Maggie continued CPR until the ambulance, driven by Maggie's husband, arrived.

Frank walked slowly away. He was in pain. He was leaning forward and his left arm was hanging. He looked toward his truck for his boy but all he could see was the sun reflecting brightly off the windshield. He waved, and despite the pain he felt radiating down his arm he could still sense the absence of his wedding ring. It did not seem to matter how long he'd gone without wearing it, like a small Gollum his thumb continued to search for the gold band that once wrapped around the underside of his finger, as if the ring and its promise could one day return. He forced his thumb to rest. His thoughts moved on toward the conversation he soon must have with his boy, about the danger of wearing waders in tidal water. He looked to the landscape which was brighter now, warmer. The boy dropped out of the black pickup and ran to his father's side.

"I feel like hammered shit," he told his son.

"You look like it, too." The boy smiled.

"God! Where were you guys!" Frank could hear Maggie yelling at her husband while two medics attended to the old man. "You stop at a bar?" Everyone called him BUD. "Me and Frank," she continued. "*That* Frank," she pointed out with her finger. "We stuck with him all the way but I think he went into cardiac arrest when his feet couldn't find bottom. When he was still in the water. I think he drowned before he got to shore."

"Obviously."

"I mean dead." Frank wanted to listen so he told Chance to go back to the truck to turn off the emergency flashers.

"Leave that for us to decide," BUD told his wife, though she knew full well that he'd have little, if anything, to do with the official report.

"A lot of his family are here."

"That it then?"

Before BUD left Maggie he saw that Frank had been watching them so he walked over with his hand out, but Frank looked at the ground as if he hadn't noticed. However, BUD kept coming. "I hear you're the accomplice helped my wife kill that old bird," Bud laughed. "You're the only guy went mouth-to-mouth with the same guy my wife did! Whatta you say about that? Huh?"

"First I'd say you were lying--I never kissed you. Then I'd say I didn't kiss the old man, either-- not like Frank kissed your wife."

"What?"

Frank already regretted saying anything at all to BUD. He didn't like having to talk to him, and he didn't like having to listen to him, especially in front of Maggie. It only made it that much harder to think of them together. How a guy like that could charm one so hardy yet elegant as Maggie was beyond Frank's comprehension. He knew they didn't have children so it wasn't a forced marriage. BUD didn't deserve Maggie, not now. Perhaps he never did. Perhaps no one did, or even could. He knew it wouldn't have been she who turned him into what was now standing here on the beach, just another big white guy in a sweaty shirt with a bad mustache, trying to look more important than he really was.

BUD kept looking at Frank while Frank looked at Maggie. "His name was Frank," Frank finally said.

"Yeah. Just like yours. Good thing Maggie

knew how t'tell you guys apart."

"Yeah...well he was the one who was dead, so...."

"I'm just kidding—just giving you a hard time. All in fun, right? If you take this job too seriously it'll kill ya." Then BUD looked to Maggie. "But she loves me. God help her, she can't help herself."

"She might surprise you," Frank said. He couldn't help himself. He could only hope.

"What?" the MEDIX driver replied. But Frank was already gone.

Back in the truck Chance waited for his dad's return. When he saw him stop and lean against the front bumper he jumped out to greet him. "So, did the old man die?" The man stood before the boy, leaning hard into his empty pockets, peering into his son's young sea-green eyes. Then he had to close his own eyes to shut out the pain. "I mean, the man's not dead, right Dad?" With his eyes closed, the man was struck by his son's small voice, how similar it was to how his mother's used to be.

"Never mind that."

"I'm hungry!"

"I need a minute."

"Maybe that's the reason we got here late today, Dad. So you could save that man's life."

"We weren't that late." The man's voice was soft now, too, not more than a whisper. Even he was surprised at his sudden weakness.

"We were right on time to save that guy. Things happen for a reason." The man thought his boy was sounding even more like his mother.

"That...doesn't sound like you." The man was having trouble talking.

"You ok, Dad? Your heart bothering you?"

"Just...out of breath," he said. "I need your shoulder. I need to lie down. Back of the truck." The man stood up and put his right arm around the boy's shoulder while leaning equally on his left, sliding his left hand along the side of the truck. "You and me," the man said and he pushed two crossed fingers on his right hand around the boy's neck into the boy's view. "We stay like this. Ok?" Then he let go of his son and held with both hands to the tailgate.

The young boy put down the gate and helped his father slide back into the truck's bed. The man kicked off what he now remembered were his most comfortable pair of sport shoes, the ones that allowed his feet to feel quick and nimble. The leather and the foot bedding were soaked with seawater and inside the toes they were heavy with wet sand.

A cough interrupted the man's thoughts. It tore through his throat and shot a dull pain down his left arm. Again he coughed, this time from a deeper place, this time two long dragging jags that squeezed all the energy from him. He felt like he was full of seawater. When he quit convulsing he recognized the points of his son's elbows driving down into his thighs. He was standing between his father's knees, where the man's lower legs dangled down off the tailgate. The boy reached out the remains of a warm orange soda.

"Much obliged," the man said, accepting the sticky orange can. He forced his head up high enough to take a swig. He returned the can then fell down again onto his back, where he immediately began to feel better. He reached overhead toward the cab and tried to lift the gallon jug of warm tap water. He always brought fresh water to rinse the tacky feel of the salt ocean from his hands and feet.

His plan had been to wash those of his boy first, as well as his arms and legs, before taking care of his own. But his thoughts were interrupted by his inability to lift the water jug. The familiar pain pressed like nails into his arm pit. Often, if he felt it coming soon enough, he could lie down to wait it out. But it never felt this bad before. He'd never tried to ignore it this long. He thought he was in the right place now to recover and he lowered his arms to rest beside his legs. According to form, his shallow breathing began to deepen. He'd had a lung collapse years before, decades before, while in college, three times, for no apparent reason. He remembered the sound of liquid bubbling in his chest, like blowing air through a straw under water, but there was no bubbling now when he breathed, even though the pain was similar. He'd never had pain quite like this in his armpit before. The needle had never gone this deep. It was like someone had stuck a long thin sliver up under his arm.

The boy was nearly as familiar with the recovery process as the man was. The boy knew better than to speak to his mother about it. He crawled up the back of the pickup and sat close to minister whatever comforts he could. He crawled up into the bed and stretched out his neck to give his father a kiss.

"Thanks, Cowboy."

"Your heart still hurting you?"

"Sometimes things hurt like they won't ever end." Frank's breath was returning, the pain was beginning to subside. "Sometimes things only hurt to tell you something's wrong. That there's something you'd better get looked at."

"You going to get it looked at?" The boy placed the warm palm of his hand on his father's cheek.

"You're scratchy. You have sand on your face. Shall I take it off?"

"I guess someone has to do it. Might as well be you. How'd your hands get so dang big anyway? Pretty soon…you won't need me to give you a hand anymore."

"That won't happen. Never and forever."

"Promises, promises. See if I care." Chance gently swept the dried white sand from his father's face. He started working his hair with his fingers as he tried to get the sand out of there too. "Damned hearts," the man said. "Can't live with'em…."

"Can't live without'em," the boy continued. "Just like women!"

Then the man got to coughing again. He spit into a piece of paper and saw there was blood so he crumpled up the paper and put it in his pocket. His breathing continued to deepen, showing a greater measure between each rise and fall of his chest. The cable was loosening its grip—that's how he described his pain. He said it felt like a thin cable wrapped around both his heart and lungs and both ends were being pulled so tight that it felt like all would be cut into halves. But they never did. Not yet.

His breathing was natural again, but he knew better than to move. Not before the sliver pulled from his armpit. He looked at the boy then looked at the jug of water.

"Right here, in the old kisser." He opened his mouth wide and the boy did his best not to spill. The man rinsed his mouth then swallowed the water, half at a time. His lungs felt heavy, thick within his chest, as if when he swallowed the water fell into his lungs, but he did not cough this time.

"So what now, Dad?"

"It's worse than before."

"I know but, can't we play a game or something? We could make things out of clouds."

"You go first. I'll rest my eyes. More water please." As soon as the boy finished pouring and lowered the jug the man's coughing began again, but this time it didn't stop. He was red in the face and blue veins rose like swollen rivers in his neck and hands. He looked to the sky and took in a long slow pull of breath then lay back again determined not to breathe, not till he absolutely had to. His lungs felt hot within. It crossed his mind that this must be how old Frank felt when the water first invaded his lungs. Then he stumbled into a place in his mind that felt something like water, if only because his head was swimming.

Now is the time for the ride of your life
warm air shivering over a barebacked horse
wind and speed and time a-bouncing
green and silver water clashing
splashing like blue grass bustling
rustling down around your feet....

Half an hour passed and the man was still asleep. Chance had not once disturbed him. A dog sounded within the man's dreams. It walked up and laid down in his pocket, and he woke.

"It's for you," he said, so the boy reached in to retrieve the cell phone. "She must've heard about the drowning accident. Why do you think she doesn't call your phone to talk to you?" The man tried not to mumble. He rubbed his eyes and noticed the pain beneath his armpit had disappeared.

"Hi, Mom. Hold on, Mom." The boy covered the phone's mouth piece tightly and leaned toward his father and whispered. "You were dreaming."

"Was I?"

"You were twitching and jerking like a dog in its sleep. You were trying to talk."

"I was?"

"And Dad? You even farted."

"I thought that was the horse."

"What horse?"

"Good for you son."

"You mad?"

"No. I was back in some dream I was having. Since you reminded me that I'd had one."

While the boy addressed his mother's multitude of questions the man stayed down trying not to hear the woman's voice. Instead, he aimed his eyes and his thoughts toward the sky where the clouds were so white and sheer they appeared blue.

In his life he'd endured being shot as a child when hunting with his father. He'd suffered bone fractures in his arm and broken blood vessels in his feet from playing sports. He'd survived bicycle and motorcycle accidents, even a car accident in high school where he'd escaped injury despite his Mustang rolling over. He'd been stuck in the eye from a branch on a rolling log while in grade school and he'd had lung surgery while still in college. And now he was passing through his second divorce with a heart that was doing a different kind of failing. And he had no idea how anything was going to turn out.

The quiet blue plane of sky above was broken by white and gray gulls blowing over him. The breeze was light and the occasional sound of whispering rose up from the sliding silver waves. Behind the ambulance that still rested on the beach old Frank's family sat in their cars beneath a new and crushing weight.

Had the man taken marriage for granted? Of course he did. Had the man intended for his wives to leave him? No. Did they? Yes. For him there were still subterranean depths yet to be plumbed, where good spirits didn't falter for better and for worse.

Most of the clam diggers that had lined the beach from north to south were now gone, leaving behind a place blemished by their digging, like so many wounds in a minefield. But in less time than it took to dig them the shallow spread of the rising tide filled them, closed them, healed them all, one by one.

Tucked behind the gallon jug of water, in the front corner of the truck's bed, the man saw an empty plastic pop bottle which would have meant nothing to him except it was filled with a quarter sand and three quarters water. He sat up, reached to the bottle and pulled it close enough to see a small marine animal, as small as a fingernail, lying on a sandy underwater island. It was not moving. He carefully put the bottle back. When the boy ended the phone call with his mother the man looked to him. The boy's eyes were filled with clouds pure and white.

"So what's in the bottle, Skipper?"

"Oh. While you were resting…. Before I forget, Hope needs a ride home."

"Her name's Maggie."

"I know. I told Maggie it was ok. Giving her a ride. But it's taking such a long time--I mean, the ambulance and all. It's still here."

"Tell me about your little animal in the bottle. It looks dead."

"Oh. While you were resting. I found a hydra! And it's perfect timing because I can take it to school tomorrow."

"A hydra?"

"It's a small marine animal, a cousin to the jellyfish—*the jellies*, as my teacher calls them, which always makes me hungry."

"It looks dead."

"No, it just looks that way. See, that's the thing. Hydras are a-maaazing creatures. Y'know, you can put one in a blender and when you pour it back out it will re-assemble itself into a new LIVING HYDRA! My teacher says they're immortal. I think it could be the coolest living thing ever, and I just love it!" Then, Maggie's voice.

"I will trade you all my clams plus half the tea in China for your magic little bean, Mr. Rain Man."

"Hi Mags," the boy said. He had become more familiar with Maggie than when Frank had last seen them together.

"Sorry t'keep you boys waiting. Ready when you are."

"We've been talking." The man was happier to see Maggie than he could admit.

"About stuff," the boy added.

"Guy stuff," the man concluded.

"Oh, is that all," she said, looking at the man. "I thought it might've been something more important. Cause that little one over there with all the brains and arms and legs is puh-retty sharp." She poked the boy in the ribs. "By the way...Hydra sounds like a girl."

"Um...it's *actually* both," the boy said.

"How can you tell if it's a boy and a girl?" Maggie asked.

"Careful, he might show you," the man said. "I hear we're taking you home. Critter, here, asked if we can keep you." The boy grabbed one of his father's outreached hands while Maggie grabbed the other and they pulled him from the truck's bed. He now stood slapping and swiping sand from his clothes.

"Chance tells me you haven't been feeling so good."

"I'm ok," the man said.

Maggie kicked at a sticker adhered to the truck's rear bumper. "Real nice. Did you put this here, kid? Betcha did. Dollars to doughnuts?"

"Then hand over the doughnuts," the boy said.

"Mmmmm…a doughnut sure sounds good about now. Whatta you say, Frank? If little boy handsome is real nice maybe the good looking man will stop at a bakery."

"Mayyy-be...if YOUUU'RE real nice," the boy said to Maggie, and all three laughed, not knowing what else to do.

"So whose bumper sticker is this? I have a bumper sticker, too." The anti-tourist bumper stickers could be seen occasionally about town on local work rigs and monster trucks. It said, THANKS FOR COMING NOW GO HOME, in black and white. "Well of course it's yours, isn't it, Frank?" Then Maggie leaned over to whisper privately into his ear. "Your new girlfriend give that to ya?"

"And Dad? Under your eyes it's purple as a black and blue mark."

"North or south?" the man asked Maggie, now driving, momentarily ignoring his son.

"North. Don't forget we need doughnuts." Maggie thought the boy would certainly second her motion, but when she looked in the back seat she found that he was already asleep.

"I like it when you say *WE*," the man said. "It makes me feel like you and I are still part of something."

"What did WE learn through being divorced?" Maggie asked.

"Smart ass. More than I wanted. Maybe nothing. Don't really know yet. But this divorce isn't over. Not yet anyway."

"Is he really asleep?"

"He's been known to fake it, but I'd say by the bounce of his head and the drool of his cheek he is indeed asleep."

"When you going to see the doc? Chance told me all about your little episode back there. You might not want to acknowledge it as such, but that's pretty bat shit crazy, Frank. Especially for him. No matter how good he seems to take it, he's having a hard time. You notice he bites his nails? I know you wouldn't want him to ignore his heart if it was him, but that's what you're teaching him to do. I'm just saying...." The truck was leaving the beach. Maggie reached back to hold the boy's head as the truck rattled up the wash board easement. "So, broken cords in your heart, huh? Is that right?"

"Just one."

"Just one, he says. I think you have something else wrong with you."

"A lot of people think that."

"What does your daughter think?" But the man had nothing to say. "That's what I thought. You haven't even talked to her, have you? I bet she doesn't even know. Because you know if she did you'd have to do something about it. Take a right, right here." What Frank really thought about his heart was that if he chose to have it looked at it would be like saying he wanted to keep the life he had, but he didn't.

"We're starting to sound like an old married couple," he said. "But I don't remember our honeymoon? Do you?"

"Yeah, I remember. You were so excited you died of a heart attack. And don't lie to me. Don't tell me you have one lung when it's the only heart you'll ever have that's breaking down. Boy Wonder told me you didn't want his mom to know because she might keep him away from you. He thought if he told me I'd help take care of you. So that's what I'm trying to do."

"Got it," the man said. He didn't feel like talking anymore.

"Right here, Frank. This is me." He looked at her too quickly, too ready for her to invite him to go somewhere alone with her. Anywhere. This made him realize just how anxious he was, just how much he wanted Maggie to want him. "This is my house."

The man slowly brought his truck to a stop. Maggie opened and closed her door quietly. Her truck was now parked in her driveway, the one with the bumper sticker that got her so much attention: THE ONLY BUSH I TRUST IS MY OWN. It had caricatures of both George Sr. and George Jr. sporting beards. "How did you get to the beach this morning?" the man asked.

The sun was hot and bright and people on holiday were mowing their yards and thinking about the leaves that soon would fall. Maggie spoke through the opened passenger window.

"A friend brought my rig home for me when I got tangled up with you at the beach. Don't go away, Frank." Maggie walked from the passenger side around the hood and leaned through the man's window until their shoulders touched. She put her left hand on his left forearm. He wanted dearly to look at her. He wanted to touch her. He wanted to see her see him looking into her eyes. But he couldn't face her.

"One step at a time," she said, holding the right side of his face with her left hand. She turned his head toward her. "Step One. Go see your doctor." Maggie was standing outside with the big blue sky behind her. Her red hair was washing softly around her face, exposing the last summer breezes that were racing between the shadows. In the man's eyes she saw the same clouds that he had seen earlier drifting through his son's eyes. Her hand lay softly on his cheek, then she let her fingertips run like cool water down his face, trickling over his lips. Her hand kept running till it flowed down his arm. When her fingers reached his elbow she started to lean away. The man reached out his hand. Just as their fingers were to lose contact Maggie spoke. "Don't forget the doughnuts," she said. Then she walked away.

"Maggie," the man called after her. "What else do we need?"

"We can always use milk," she laughed. "And for Pete's sake buy a razor—you should know by now I don't like mustaches. They're so...."

"Porno?" the man suggested.

"Exactly."

OF DUST AND THE RIVER

Three hours without a bump and the sturgeon fishermen grew drunk and bored and ill tempered. They pulled anchor and motored back across the Columbia River toward the Oregon shore. They trailered the boat then dropped it at the owner's home before moving on to breakfast.

At the cafe the men talk about the one that got away, managing their story according to superstition. How big the fish was. How high it jumped. What one another did wrong that allowed the sturgeon to break free. The story grows to be as fantastic as their expectations had been prior to that morning's launch. They do not speak about their catch, one undersized fish. They rail on about the tourists, how the declining state of the fishery is their fault, how they come from the big cities with their money and skim the cream off the top of what they, the locals, fight year round to preserve. The three men speak loudly enough to influence two tables in Maggie's section to leave before they are through.

"Don't worry," the boat owner says. "We'll tip ya double."

"Triple's what's fair," Maggie says. "Any you

jerks want more coffee?" The three fishermen nod and laugh and lean away from their empty cups.

"It really burns my butt. How we got to hide undersized fish. Just so those jokers got another place to spend their money."

"I know, Hon—but tell your wife. She'll kiss it, not me."

"I'd let you," he says. "Hell, I'd even kiss yours," he adds, and he places before her a look of promise, of desire. But the look is tired, and the winning smile is showing wear.

"Maybe..." she says, leaning closer. Not much closer. Now close. "Maybe I'm the one should tell your wife."

For three full seconds the boat owner holds Maggie's eyes. "Mags?" he says.

"Hmmm?" But her look has gone sour.

"Nothin."

"Good boy. Now any you slobs want dessert?"

While the three men consume pie and coffee their catch, one illegal sturgeon, lies in a wheelbarrow gasping for air in a dark garage, a knife stuck into its head. In the driveway is the boat, water still trickling out the back. Pieces of broken smelt dry on the hot seats in the sun, shrinking, hardening against the vinyl. Beside the wheelbarrow a six-year-old boy stands, jawing back at the sturgeon as it plies its gills against the dry thin air. Inside the garage it is musty and cool, smelling of dust and the river.

When the gills move the eyes move also. The boy reaches out with one tentative finger, but the mouth suddenly flexes and he quickly draws back his arm. From beside the garage the boy rips up a handful of dandelions. He returns to the wheelbarrow and begins to investigate the eyes and gills with a single long stem. Into the wide toothless mouth the boy carefully places one yellow blossom.

The boy's mother appears from within the house. She scolds him for torturing the fish and tells him to return inside. The boy leaves without a word, but rather than going into the house he climbs upon an overturned bucket outside the garage to watch his mother through a dirt-streaked window.

The woman tries unsuccessfully to withdraw the knife from the sturgeon's head. Each time she tries to dislodge the blade she inadvertently lifts the head and the tail begins to scratch and thrash at its confinement. She hoists her foot into the wheelbarrow but then refuses to hold its head down in this way. Without questioning whether or not she has the conviction to end the fish's suffering the woman grabs up the only other knife available, a fillet knife. She begins stabbing at the fish's head, trying to avoid hitting the sturgeon's open eyes. But the sturgeon's head is too thick for the flimsy tip of the fillet knife to pierce. All her blows glance miserably away, cutting the gray skin, marking it with white cuts that begin to bleed.

Along one wall there is a work bench and a collection of tools. The man's wife angrily takes up a screwdriver which turns out to be less effective than the fillet knife. Her hands begin to shake. She gets a bigger screwdriver and a small hammer with which to hit it, but she cannot land the hammer squarely without hitting her fingers. The fish is writhing against the wheelbarrow, its skin scraping roughly against the metal, its gills and mouth are flexing. Its open eyes move. The woman is not angry at the fish.

She stands at her husband's tool bench considering the nails, the larger hammers and saws. She fixes for a moment on a folding camp shovel but then moves on. Her eyes keep coming back to a hand sickle that she's used in the yard. Her fingers wrap tightly round the dark wooden grip. Before she can drop the first blow she hears her son's voice beside her.

"Try this," he says, and he hands her one of her good kitchen knives. He points to a spot on the sturgeon's skull, an inch from being symmetrically opposite the point where his father's knife remains. "Try not to stab," he says softly. "Use your hand." He takes each of her hands and sets them into place. He demonstrates how to use the heel of her right hand to hit against the butt end of the knife. The boy then turns and goes to the house.

After killing the fish the woman steps back and for the first time begins to see what she has done. She looks down at the unmoving body, no longer feeling desperate in her sympathy. In fact, she is hardly sympathetic at all now. It is just a fish. Until she notices the bright yellow dandelion within its mouth. Then she considers what gender the fish might be. She has no way of knowing, but the flower prompts her to think it is female. Just a feeling. An intuition, maybe. She plucks the flower from the cold, still mouth, and on her way back to the house it accidentally drops into the grass. The blossom is so delicate she does not feel it leave her hand.

She moves slowly now, quietly, removing herself to the bathroom where she self-consciously washes her hands and her face and her arms. She begins to pour a bath, not for herself but for her son. Not too hot. It has been a long time since she has given her son a bath. He had grown out of needing her for that. She is prepared to cover him with a cloth if he has also grown too modest for her eyes, and she pours shampoo under the faucet to create a thin white veil of cloaking bubbles. As she calls to him she begins to remember how it was before she returned to work—to help pay for the house and the truck and the new sturgeon boat, thinking to help carry her family to the next better thing. As her son appears in the doorway, a curiosity of eyes and ears and elbows, she reaches for him and feels how big he has grown. In the boy's face she foresees the stories her husband will tell upon his return, about those fish that got away, and she forces herself to close her eyes. There she sits for quite some time, knees down upon the bathroom floor, almost content, until the boy leaves her tight embrace.

ACKNOWLEDGEMENTS

Thanks to Polly June, Ms. Bane, Father Bob, and to Babs. And kudos to Bubs for reminding me not to forget you. Thanks to Katie for believing. Thanks to Donna who shoots a camera like a gun, and to Sandra--a Canuck who shoots a gun like a true American. Thanks to Pig and to Granny--the last of the Necanicum Hillbillies. To Holly Lorincz for her guidance and to the Filthy Five who once led me astray. Thanks to those peddling my coffee so I can peddle my books, and to those groundbreakers still minding the homestead, and to my three lost brothers and our sister. Thanks of course to my kids, Autumn and Jacob, who constantly remind me that, "That's not how it happened, at all." And thanks to Nancy, mother of my children, who one way or another has influenced each one of these first stories.